Drowning the
Gowns

COMHAIRLE CHONTAE ÁTHA CLIATH THEAS
SOUTH DUBLIN COUNTY LIBRARIES

COUNTY LIBRARY, TOWN CENTRE, TALLAGHT
TO RENEW ANY ITEM TEL: 462 0073
OR ONLINE AT www.southdublinlibraries.ie

Items should be returned on or before the last date below. Fines, as displayed in the Library, will be charged on overdue items.

DROWNING THE GOWNS
First published in 2016
by
New Island Books,
16 Priory Hall Office Park,
Stillorgan,
County Dublin.
Republic of Ireland.

www.newisland.ie

PRINT ISBN: 978-1-84840-497-7
EPUB ISBN: 978-1-84840-498-4
MOBI ISBN: 978-1-84840-499-1

British Library Cataloguing Data.
A CIP catalogue record for this book is available from the British Library.

Typeset by JVR Creative India
Cover design by Mariel Deegan
Printed by ScandBook AB, Sweden

New Island is grateful to have received financial assistance from The Arts Council of Northern Ireland (1 The Sidings, Antrim Road, Lisburn, BT28 3AJ, Northern Ireland).

LOTTERY FUNDED

10 9 8 7 6 5 4 3 2 1

To my children:
Kate, Jack and Rebecca.

'Venice has been painted and described many thousands of times, and of all the cities of the world is the easiest to visit without going there.'

– Henry James, *Italian Hours*

'Kublai Khan does not necessarily believe everything Marco Polo says when he describes the cities visited on his expeditions, but the emperor of the Tartars does continue listening to the young Venetian with greater attention and curiosity than he shows any other messenger or explorer of his.'

– Italo Calvino, *Invisible Cities*

Part One:
Ponte di Donna Onesta

1.

Venice was not Italy.
It was not anywhere.

It floated above its own reflection in the water; a palimpsest city.

It looked like a crannóg now to Reuben Ross as he crossed the laguna, struggling to row one-oared the skiff he had borrowed that morning from Tito. The Venetians were beginning to illuminate early evening lanterns in the maws of windows, their twins glimmering in the water. Only then did it come home to him how late it was, how long he had laboured on the shore of the island of St George of the Seaweed, attempting to easel paint the watery city from that particular vantage point. He worried about what he would find on his canvas with the morrow's daylight: the curves, squares, flat planes and arcs of the concrete city would be there all right, but somehow his gaze and brushes had been increasingly drawn to the insubstantial iridescence of the aqueous other city, the shifting, blurring colours and patterns, with the ripples and brief creases the wind made coming off

3

the mountains and crazing the water like craquelure. He was altogether unsure what sort of image he was bearing back with him into the city.

Now it was all smoke and mirrors on the water with the first veils of early evening mist closing in and causing a strange stillness to descend. It was why he had stopped rowing and was standing on the poop of the skiff gazing at the lights coming on, and how he heard the voices carrying quite clearly across the water.

Although he could not distinguish the actual words, the sense he made of the sound was of such urgency he could not prevent himself from turning his head in their direction. So doing, he could see two men balancing in a gondola that rose and fell lightly some distance to his port side. In truth, Reuben was briefly glad to be distracted, both from the baffling view of Venice and also from the toil of handling the oar. Tito, a boatman, had instructed him all summer with his *lezeoni di voga*[1], but it remained an alien, awkward operation, very different from the youthful rowing he had done on the Leitrim lakes.

Gazing in the direction of the gondola, his idle inquisitiveness shifted quite suddenly to concern. For, as he watched, the smaller of the two men seemed to perform for him an act of prodigious strength. Reaching into the low, dark *felze*[2] of the vessel, this figure lifted out a female form, which he promptly, with no great exertion, deposited over the side into the lagoon.

Such was the shock that Reuben had to steady himself and his skiff too with the oar. Aghast, he watched as the man repeated the operation, this time discarding what seemed a second female figure over the gunwale facing Reuben.

The lack of surface disturbance, however, and of any accompanying sound of a splash, began to lessen Reuben's unease about these bizarre proceedings, turning his interest once more to curiosity. The man appeared to be disposing of garments overboard. The garments refused to fill with water and submerge. The second man on board, evidently the gondolier, was the first to spot this, and he proceeded to point the circumstance out to his companion. Agitated, the passenger gestured to the boatman, who moved forward and began to spear the floating clothes with his oar, using it like a giant laundry stick. This action caused the gondola to rock from side to side and almost plunge the passenger head first into the floating gowns, for such the garments were, ballooned with air, their sleeves floating like waving wraith-like limbs.

Enthralled, Reuben watched as the gowns refused to sink, their buoyant, shadowy forms insisting on rising to the surface so that dark mermaids seemed to encircle the bobbing gondola. Then, raising his eyes again, there was the jolt of a second shock.

The two men were looking at him.

They had momentarily ceased their efforts with the floating gowns; they had straightened up to stare at him.

Reuben was greatly disconcerted at being thus discovered. For all he knew, the disposal of a real body had preceded the dumping of the gowns. And even if such were not the case, he felt as if he had intruded upon an intensely private, clandestine event not meant for his eyes.

So he forced himself into action. Putting his back into it, he began to row the skiff, trying in his anxiety not to dislodge the oar from the intricately notched *fórcola*[3] and so halt his progress or, worse, lose the oar overboard. It occurred to him as he rowed that, if they chose to pursue him, the experienced gondolier would have little difficulty catching up and overtaking him, cutting off his safe return to the city. Looking hurriedly around him, it chilled him to see no other water traffic: he was quite alone apart from the two men in the gondola.

Out of breath, he paused at one point to check behind him, but the gondola was still bobbing in the area where he had first spied it. The men were not in chase.

Reuben did not slacken his effort, however, and at length he glided under the shadow of the *Casa degli Spiriti*, and was relieved to lose himself and his canvas in the city's dark maze of canals and waterways. Checking over his shoulder, all he spied were a few stray tendrils of mist curling, unfurling, ghostlike in his wake.

2.

Reuben had never made love fully clothe-less before Venice.

In Ireland it had been outhouses: some fumbling and clumsy assignations. In England, too cold. The lady in Paris had deemed exposure unsightly and unseemly so that afterwards they straightened and rearranged their garments before sleep.

It was Gina, whom Signor Grimaldi procured as a model for him, who introduced him to this franker form of lovemaking. At first, however, he had difficulties with it: his nakedness distracted him and put a check to any arousal on his part. This unease angered Gina, and he did not see her for a couple of days. When eventually she reappeared at the rooms he rented in the Canareggio district of the city, one of which had a window large enough to double as his studio, she warned him of the Norwegian artist who was looking for a model. He apologised to her, though she still glowered at him.

– Yet, she argued, it is not a problem for you to see me without my clothes!

– That's work, he half-protested, and then, thinking better of it, conceded. But you're right. I should not be so ashamed of my nakedness.

Nevertheless, that next time still required the tantalising touch of the tip of her tongue on his, the slight bite of her nails on his chest, and the light brush of her fingertips along his thighs, and upwards, for all to go well.

– Now, she assured him. When you paint me, people will blush.

Reuben had been lying on his side, listening to her; now he rolled over onto his back.

– Are all Irish boys like this? she enquired, gazing at him.

– No, he replied. I do not think so.

That night, while she slept beside him, he studied the chalky, canvas pallor of his own outstretched body in the gloom of the bedroom. He could make out the muscled tone of his stomach and his long, strong legs. Already lean before leaving Ireland, he realised now that he had lost more weight; his form seemed oddly angular, with his hips protrusive and his ribcage faintly visible. Then, feeling suddenly cold and exposed, he reached down and pulled the striped blanket up around him.

From Reuben's café table outside Florian's, in the Piazza San Marco, he studied now the halo of shadow that encased a gentleman's head and shoulders where he strolled across the almost empty square, shading himself with a parasol. The *flâneur*[4] had come to his attention because, at one point, the smooth rhythm of his passage had been disrupted when he tripped on some uneven paving stones in the middle of the piazza. Reuben had accompanied Gina to the piazza and had watched her disappear with the crowd of other celebrants into the great basilica before taking his place at the café and ordering some coffee for himself, intending to wait there until her Mass ended. After four months in Venice the sight of men with parasols and fans still bemused him, but now it was the composition of this cone of shadow that engrossed him, for he swore it looked almost vermillion in hue, not the black he had been assuming every shadow to be.

A figure suddenly blocked his view of the parasol-passerby, and a man's voice intruded on his reverie.

– You are not observing devotions then? the man enquired of him, nodding in the direction of the church. You are Irish, are you not?

– Yes, Reuben said, sitting up as he suddenly realised who his interlocutor was. But not that Irish.

– Ah! I've grown up rather pewless myself: my father brought us up not theologically *en règle*[5], as it were. We could plead, he would assure us, the whole privilege of Christendom, and that there was no communion, even that of the Catholics, even that of the Jews, even that of the Swedenborgians, from which we need find ourselves excluded.

The man smiled nervously at this point, and indicated enquiringly the vacant seat at Reuben's table.

– I must confess I've never found the inclination to test his assertion. I do not mean to impose, but I find I must speak with you. May I?

Without really waiting for an invitation from Reuben, the man took his seat and looked cautiously around him. There were not many other clients at the neighbouring tables, and for the moment a waiter was nowhere to be seen. Once settled he reached up and removed his hat, the brim of which had sat level with his eyebrows. Piercing grey eyes were thus revealed, and Reuben suddenly found himself the object of their direct gaze.

– You no doubt know me, sir.

– Of course I do, Reuben too readily assured him.

The American writer had been pointed out to him on several occasions, most recently on a visit to the Accademia by Dalglish, a Scottish illustrator and engraver with whom he had become friendly. Now, at close quarters, Reuben took in a middle-aged man of robust build, but becoming corpulent. His forehead was rendered more pronounced by a receding hairline, and he had an almost aquiline nose, were it not for a short bend that Reuben's artist's eye detected. He dressed like an Englishman, and Reuben suspected that the white shirt he wore was intended to counterpoint the dark brown beard that seemed to hide the bottom half of his face. A royal-blue bow tie interacted well with those gray discs of his eyes.

Reuben's spontaneous admission of recognition, however, had the effect of forming a confused frown on the wide dome of the man's forehead, and the gray gaze seemed to intensify until he gave a sudden half-smile of comprehension, which relaxed the writer's features. He softly shook his head.

– You mean you know me by reputation, do you not?

Now it was Reuben's turn to frown with confusion.

– I have of course read and admired your work, if that is what you mean, sir.

Reuben wondered at a writer of such stature still in need of affirmation. The writer held up his hand.

– Forgive me. Thank you for your kind comments, but I am not in pursuance of flattery.

A waiter arrived, and Reuben agreed to a glass of Valpolicella, then they sat silently the while until they were served. The writer sat up and leaned forwards for privacy's sake as a man had sat down close by, cooling himself with what appeared to be a fan of ostrich feathers.

– I mean from the other night. You do not know to link me with the other night?

– The other night? Reuben repeated, and then the picture began to form for him. Spotting this dawning in his features, the man sat back and nodded his head.

– The escapade, the writer termed it in a low voice, though he seemed to mull this term over before rephrasing it as: that horrid predicament on the laguna.

– Good Lord, Reuben exclaimed. That was you!

The man with the fan sat up in a kind of reflex of shock and looked around sternly at them.

3.

– You must think me some Bluebeard, the writer resumed, although the deep sadness of mien undid any intended light-heartedness.

Reuben was still gaping somewhat at the revelation that it had been the writer doing the disposing of the gowns. The writer had evidently, to judge by his comment, been able to conjure up the perspective of an unwitting observer coming across what must have seemed a macabre spectacle.

– It was an extraordinary sight. Reuben felt prompted to confirm his impressions for the writer. A little unsettling if you must know. However, if no crime was committed it is no longer any real business of mine.

– No crime. The writer seemed to savour the words, rolling them around his tongue. No. Crime.

The two of them sat a while in silence as if in contemplation of the phrase; Reuben took the opportunity to taste the wine. The writer then shook himself from the reverie into which he had momentarily lapsed and took the subject up again.

– No murder or personal injury took place, upon my honour. Please be assured. And you are correct: the whole thing is an intensely private matter involving a fine, dearly departed Lady. Her reputation and her family's peace of mind are all bound up with the silly incident. It is why I have taken the liberty to seek you out. To track you down, as it were.

For a second time, Reuben found himself the object of the writer's piercing gaze.

– You have, it seems, set in train a series of enquiries with reference to the evening in question, and it is my desire to explain enough of the incident to set your mind at ease and bring to a term your own investigations. To, as it were, put a lid on things.

– I did not go to the authorities, Reuben interrupted, if that is your worry.

What he had done was relate the whole incident to Tito, who, being a waterman, was confident that by merely asking around he would soon discover the name of the gondolier who had been the accomplice in the affair, and so bring to light the identity, purpose and intent of the second man. Tito's investigations had not, it seemed, gone unnoticed.

– I impressed upon my boatman the need to be discreet.

– Hah! The writer practically guffawed, inducing the fan-man to look disapprovingly around once more. Discreet! Venice is a voice, he insisted. The Venetians are a vocal race.

Here he waved his hand in the general direction of the piazza, intending it to act as proxy for the whole city.

– Venetians exchange confidences at a distance of half a mile. Don't you see how it's brought me to you the opposite way? How I've discovered you? A painter. Irish. Making a living from the local burghers' wives.

Reuben gave this declaration his somewhat shocked attention.

– You've been making your own enquiries.

The words came out with the force of an accusation.

– The canals criss-cross and interconnect. It's a giant web. Start a ripple in one and it becomes a pulse in another, a revelation in a third. Your 'Tito' will soon enough know about me, and you will be able to confound him by being privy to the information before him.

– I see, returned Reuben. Then, after another moment: and am I to know then what it is you put a lid on?

The yellow-sounding bells of the campanile began to ring at this point, causing an applause of pigeons in the square. Pedestrians seemed to pause in mid stroll, café conversations ceased. Not for the first time Reuben was struck by the sun-lit happy pealing of the bells, unlike the dour, slate-grey clarion call he often heard pulsate across the flat fields of his father's land at home. At length the writer was able to elaborate:

– I was carrying out a duty requested of me by the loved ones of the deceased to dispose of some of the Lady's belongings. She was a lady who had travelled far and accumulated many possessions; too many to ship back to America.

– But to dump them in the lagoon? There is no shortage of charitable institutions in Venice where you may have left them. The Scuola di San Rocco, for example....

The writer stiffened at this, and went pale as if in vivid contemplation of the prospect of the Lady's counterfeits let loose about the city, and the possibility of encountering one by accident evidently quite chilled and appalled the man. Motivated by what he read on the man's face, Reuben said:

– I apologise. I speak out of turn.

The writer shook his head in deprecation and then looked up at the lively bustle of the café beginning to fill up around them. This prompted him to lift his hat and leave some centesimi on the tabletop.

– We will speak again, he assured Reuben as he got up, affixing the hat's brim level once more with his eyebrows, lowering the bluish light of his eyes. Your accommodation is in the Jewish Quarter is it not?

– I hope, Reuben offered by way of replying in the affirmative, my boatman proves as well informed as yours.

At this the writer paused and smiled down at him.

– I rather doubt it. Giorgio knows everything. He quite, you see, steers my course for me.

With the curtest of bows, the writer went off, making for the plantation of *poli*[6] that marked where the main *traghetto*[7] was located and where, by shading his eyes, Reuben could just make out the rocking-horse jostle of black-lacquered poops and prows. The man was quickly lost among the crowd, though Reuben was distracted anyway by the sight of Gina coming towards him, all bright and beautiful in her Sunday finery.

– I light a candle for you, she informed him, causing him to stare up at her.

There was something about the act that made him shiver in the sunlight that was now flooding their side of the piazza.

4.

The women of the neighbourhood had hailed two workers from one of the nearby *squeri*[8], and they were now balancing on the lower level of the flight of water-steps, pulling the body from the canal. Rust-coloured water lapped their feet and the lowest step.

Two days after the meeting in San Marco, a letter had arrived at his studio in the writer's hand, and Reuben was hastening now to keep the appointment that the letter had suggested. Halted by the sight of a commotion, he approached the crowd. Before he was able to discover the reason for the gathering, he saw what struck him as a familiar figure detach itself from the far side of the onlookers and stride off down the quayside. On an impulse Reuben called after him, and was convinced the man had heard, for he appeared to stall a moment before darting into a little *calle*[9] away from the canal.

Returning his attention to the crowd, tall as he was, he had only to crane his neck to see, and immediately recoiled at the mangled sight. Here was no decorous Pre-Raphaelite Ophelia emerging from the waters, but the broken cadaver of a young woman, her torn clothes besmirched with the city's effluent, water fronds and orange peel entangled in her trailing hair.

His disquiet and confusion were not in any great way dispelled at the sight of the actual writer, minutes later, waiting for him farther along the canal, at the rendezvous point agreed by missive.

– Extraordinary, Reuben declared as he came up. I could have sworn to have just seen you mere minutes ago. Back that way. You must, sir, have a double.

– To gallivant by deputy, the writer marvelled. What a wonderful idea, he declared. But as you see I have not been in two places at one time; alas, I have been here these ten minutes. I am always prompt.

Imagining this some slight on his own timekeeping, Reuben reported the incident that had delayed him.

– How sad, the writer frowned. A young woman, you say. They often seem so troubled by countless things.

– Why, sir, you speak as if the poor wretch had taken her own life!

The writer regarded him at this, then said:

– I did not mean to infer such a thing.

And then, on further reflection, he added:

– Perhaps you are no longer in the mood?

– To see this masterpiece you mentioned in your letter? No. Please. Let's proceed. You do understand, though, that I have done the grand tour of Titians and Tintorettos,

Veroneses and Bellinis? I might be Irish but I'm not, sir, one of Mr Jonathan Swift's Yahoos.

The writer regarded him sharply in reaction to this last.

– I fear you've taken offense at my invitation. I do not, I assure you, presume to tell you your trade, much less doubt that you have done your duty by the masters you mention. You must know, however, how many a masterpiece rather mischievously plays hide-and-seek with us enthusiasts, tantalising us from the unaccommodating gloom of side chapels and sacristies located in damp-ridden churches in small, forgotten *campi*[10]. One such I merely wish to show you, he concluded.

The writer turned and indicated the gondola that awaited them. Reuben nodded, and as they proceeded to step on board, and surmising that the gondolier – a burly figure with bulging arms, no doubt the product of years plying the waterways thereabouts – was the redoubtable Giorgio, he felt prompted to quip:

– I hope you are not planning to dispose of *me*.

The writer clapped him quite suddenly and soundly on the back in appreciation of the humour, and Reuben had to grip the edge of the *felze* quickly to prevent falling overboard.

Once underway, and sitting side by side, the writer placed his hand on Reuben's arm and said:

– As for being Irish, my sister Alicia is very fond of the Irish. She is a great supporter of, indeed advocate for, Home Rule.

– And you? Reuben enquired.

– I fear it would give rise to violence, and I would not wish upon your little island the devastation visited upon my own divided nation. 'The Civil War': a curiously contradictory terminology, I have always thought. In any case, Gladstone will dither over it as he has done with Russia and the Sudan. I did attend Parnell's trial, though. What theatre! He was terrifically Miltonic, the writer enthused. Despicable what was done to him of course, although there was the perfume of the boudoir about the whole thing.

– And the forgeries, Reuben reminded him.

– All correspondences are dangerous, the writer attested. For once, though, it seemed that he valued the aphorism over expansiveness, and did not elaborate. Instead, they glided along silently in the gondola.

After a while, Reuben thought to ask his companion about his interest in the pictorial arts.

– I remember – the writer was expansive once more – when I was eleven, my brother and I visited the Louvre, and curiously my recollection was how, to my own sense, the paintings and portraits seemed to fill those vast halls with the influence rather of some complicated sound, diffused and reverberant, than of visibilities. I hear them still.

Moving at this point out onto the main canal, they merged with the colourful crush of waterborne traffic that was rocking on the swell caused by the churning of the screw of one of the *vaporettos*. These recent contraptions were more Verne than Venice, it seemed to them. They kept their counsel however, listening instead as Giorgio issued a flow of Venetian invective after the quickly disappearing steamer. At length he too fell silent, and soon had them sliding smoothly along the canal until they reached that stretch between the Foscali and the Rialto. Here Reuben commented:

– Do you know that this is the only part of the city that strikes me as having the appearance of deluge, of a city flooded? All the rest gloriously floats.

– A drowning world, the writer mused. Sounds like one of Bertie Wells's scientific romances. Look, up ahead: our disembarkation point.

Reuben could feel Giorgio steering the gondola at an angle now, aiming for a narrow *approdo*[11] that trailed down into the water. Once level with the steps, Reuben stepped lightly up onto the small *fondamenta*[12]. He turned in time to see Giorgio come forward solicitously and extend his free hand, the other still gripping the oar, and the writer automatically reach out his own, accepting the assistance to disembark. Reuben looked away.

– There can be no finer form of transportation to appear in, the writer announced, standing suddenly at his side. I always think arrival *en gondole* bestows a dignity even on the most unassuming of destinations.

They both looked around to appraise the singular vessel.

– It is hard to believe that some scholars claim that the word 'gondola' derives from the name the Greeks gave to the ferry of Charon, the writer cheerfully informed his companion.

– And yet, Reuben rejoined, they often remind me of velvet-lined versions of the canoes the savages use in the novels of your compatriot Fenimore Cooper.

After a moment, when his companion did not respond to this observation, Reuben turned, and was shocked to see the writer suddenly pale and disconcerted.

– Are you not well, sir? he enquired, wondering if he should seek some assistance from the gondolier.

The writer shook his head and, with no explanation as to the source of his disquiet, strode off suddenly into the back streets, indicating to Reuben that he should follow. Casting one last look in the direction of the bobbing gondola, he complied.

5.

Only when the couple entered the damp gloom of the Church of San Giovanni Crisostomo did the writer's spirits seem to rise. While Reuben paused to let his eyes adjust after the sunlight without, the writer was moving quickly and excitedly down the short aisle in the direction of the altar.

– It's a small canvas I admit, he was commentating back to him now, though in hushed tones. By Sebastian del Piombo. Do you know him?

– Vaguely, Reuben confessed, while aware that the writer was not really listening, being now in full flow.

– He was Venetian by birth, but few of his works are to be seen in his native place. This one represents the patron saint of this church giving audience to three female votaries.

He broke off his lecture and looked around, murmuring something about the dark. Then, spotting what he wanted, he darted off to one of the side chapels and appropriated a candle, meant more for devotion than the practical illumination for which he was lighting it. By this stage, Reuben was in place, squinting up at the painting; the writer joined him, and on tiptoes held the candle up to the image.

– Look at her, he intoned.

And they both stood and looked. In the foreground were the three votaries, dressed like Venetian ladies from the sixteenth century, but it was the foremost one who held them spellbound. While her two companions were in profile, politely waiting for the saint's attention, quite simply she had turned her head away and was looking out from the canvas, directly at them, as if their sudden appearance there had caught her attention; a reversal and subversion of the normal pact one presumed between the viewer and the object. Indeed, Reuben experienced the almost vertiginous impression of being himself the one viewed, the one under scrutiny. He quite started at his companion's voice beside him.

– Such hauteur, the writer enthused, such tranquil superiority.

– She's like a goddess, Reuben exhaled at length.

As he made his observation, the light guttered as if a door had opened somewhere in the church. It made Reuben look around, for he suddenly had the impression that they had been caught in the act of some furtive veneration. By whom? Outside the quavering circle of candlelight, the extremities of the church were shrouded in shadow. He looked up again at the luminous face, and was struck this time by the calm conviction he detected there; his gaze, no matter what the competing claim to his attention, would irrevocably return to her features.

Later, of Saint Giovanni he could recall little; only that bright disc remained imprinted on his memory. In London he had gazed directly into one of the new electrical lights, and had been alarmed by the scar to his vision of the after-image of the bulb. The votary's face seemed to glow with a similar voltage.

They had found a neighbourhood trattoria to sit at, and once the owner had chased off the local urchins, who had swarmed around his two customers, they had peace to discuss the painting.

– For all her external calmness, the writer maintained, there are troubled depths, I think, in her eyes.

– She's almost impious, Reuben stated.

– Brave of del Piombo, when you consider the Inquisition.

– You know what Veronese's defence was when he was brought in front of the Inquisitors because of his *Last Supper* for the convent of Santi Giovanni e Paolo?

– I think I do, the writer replied. But go on, remind me.

– He was questioned as to why he had included unholy figures such as the German, and therefore Protestant, halberdiers.

– And his defence?

– It was simple. He said, 'We painters use the same license as poets and madmen.'

– I had heard 'poets and jesters', although 'jesters' is a completely inadequate rendition of '*giullari*', which itself is best translated by the French '*jongleurs*'. No matter, it amounts to the same thing, the writer said.

– How did you ever discover her? Reuben asked.

– The Lady, came the simple reply.

Reuben was for the moment confused.

– Which Lady? he enquired, looking in the direction of the recently vacated church.

– Of the laguna, the writer clarified. My deeply missed, dear friend. She it was did me the immeasurable service of showing me the painting. Don't you see now what a wise and wonderful person she was? She found such treasures.

Reuben sat the while in respectful appreciation of these words. However, the writer had more to say on the subject of the Lady: he in fact referred back to the awkward moment at the *approdo*.

– Fenimore Cooper, he suddenly stated, was her relative. Your sudden reference to him quite shook me!

– I had no idea, Reuben said apologetically.

The writer made a mute gesture to reassure him. He then admitted:

– It is just that I still find it very upsetting. I so valued her intelligence, her dedication to her work. She really was a gifted writer, you know.

– You must recommend me something by her, Reuben suggested.

The writer half-turned in his seat and looked at Reuben. Eventually, he said:

– Giorgio informs me you row.

Reuben received this enquiry with a quizzical look.

– I learned to row as a child, in Ireland.

– You see, so did she, the writer expounded proudly. As a girl, in Ohio, where she grew up, on the Great Lakes. What the penny dreadfuls exult in calling the 'Wild West'. She even explored the alligator swamps of Florida, often on her own. She possessed within herself the pioneer spirit of the frontier, and brought that with her here to Europe. To Venice, indeed, for she rowed these very canals.

– Venice must really have suited her.

– Do you know Thomas Moore's ballad, 'The Lake of the Dismal Swamp'?

Reuben shook his head.

– I know 'The Minstrel Boy', he offered.

– It was a favourite of hers. Moore wrote it when visiting Virginia.

– I had no idea he even visited America, Reuben confessed.

Then, unbidden, the writer began to quote:

They made her a grave, too cold and damp
For a soul so warm and true;
And she's gone to the Lake of the Dismal Swamp,
Where, all night long, by a fire-fly lamp,
She paddles her white canoe.

– Venice perhaps suited her too much, the writer murmured then. She was prone to dark thoughts.

This brought a solemn silence down upon them, and they sat at the table, their glasses long drained.

At length, Reuben sought to lighten things.

– Well, through you she has done me the good turn of introducing me to Del Piombo's Venetian lady.

This seemed to have the required effect, for the writer laughed softly at his statement.

– Ah. It might not be such a favour. The image positively haunts you, you know. But you were impressed, were you not?

Reuben hesitated before replying, alert quite suddenly to the tone and timbre of this last enquiry. Gone now was the wistfulness and regret; replaced by the eagerness and energy that the writer had displayed in the chapel. Accordingly, Reuben turned in his seat and looked directly at his companion, who was across the table from him. After a moment, he found the form of words to voice his suspicion.

– It was a test?

The writer sat quietly a while as if weighing these words. Eventually, he said:

– Only in that others have come away unimpressed. They have not been susceptible.

– And you judge that I have been?

– Why, have not you been? The writer pressed home the point. You looked as if you had just made the acquaintance of the most dazzling of creatures; as if I had just introduced you to a great beauty at a dinner party with whom you have quite suddenly become smitten.

– Well I have, I have, Reuben laughed. After a moment he then added: and being thus 'susceptible', as you put it, qualifies me for what exactly?

The writer was looking around the empty *campo* and, ascertaining that the urchins were nowhere to be seen, he laid a few coins on the tabletop and rose from his seat.

– Shall we walk, now that the coast is clear?

As they strolled into the little latticework of lanes, he took it up again:

– You were always qualified, he assured Reuben. Rather, your reaction gives me the confidence I required to ask a service of you.

– A service? Reuben replied. Is there more disposing of things to be done? Of the Lady's affairs?

– On the contrary, in fact, the writer declared. You rather interrupted our efforts that night; convinced us quite to discontinue our activity. And so I find that I retain in my possession one of her gowns.

At this, the writer pulled up and turned to face the artist.

– I would like to commission you to do a drawing of it for me. Simply that. I'm content we can arrange a fee without imperilling our friendship.

– Of course, Reuben stammered. We can come to some agreement.

Once more, the writer surveyed around him as if getting his bearings.

– Now, he wondered, how to get back to the canal? Do you know, my young friend, in Venice nothing requires more care than not to lose the useful faculty of … getting lost. Now, let us '*andare per le fondere!*'[13]

6.

– Who is Signor Grimaldi? the writer asked him.

They had rediscovered the canal and were afloat again; Giorgio was returning Reuben to the Canareggio. It did not surprise him that the writer should have heard of Grimaldi; although his shop was located close to the Merceria, Reuben had quickly gathered that the dealer's reach and influence spread farther afield than that. He was, in truth, more *brocanteur* than *antiquario*[14], but he had acted for Reuben in the past as agent and vendor.

– He has been very helpful to me selling some of my portraits, and even securing me the odd commission.

They glided along, and the writer nodded and considered.

– Can he be trusted? he directed next at Reuben.

– He takes a commission fee, Reuben began, only to stop in mid sentence at the writer waving his hand dismissively.

– His eye, the writer interjected. I mean, do you trust his eye? His taste? Would you consider him an expert?

Reuben tried to picture the interior of Grimaldi's premises, only for the writer to appear to read his thoughts:

– I have browsed there, he related. A few interesting trinkets in the jumble of otherwise discarded flotsam; some, I might add, of dubious provenance and age, although in truth that might well be a sign of acumen and a measure of the signor's perceptiveness when it comes to the taste and gullibility of my countrymen, who quite positively besiege the city.

As this sounded like a commingling of diatribe and appreciation, Reuben thought to check:

– Has he embezzled you, sir? Did you purchase some item, perhaps?

The writer looked askance at this, and then laughed.

– Do you think me fatuous enough to buy a fake or faulty *objet*? When I have browsed the hoards of the greatest dragons of Europe? I have had entrance to, have handled and admired at close and privileged quarters indeed, the spoils of castles and chateaux; pallazios. Collections both mighty and miniature; galleries public and private; museums and menageries. In short, no: I have not been making purchases *chez* Grimaldi.

It was Reuben's turn to wave his hands in the air in mock submission to this litany-strewn rebuttal of any insinuation of a failure in taste or discernment on the part of the great writer.

– Would you say he was up to the task of evaluating the true worth of some items of furniture; of giving a fair and honest estimation of value?

Reuben considered before replying, his hesitation no aspersion on Grimaldi, but due rather to the reflection that the writer must know more reputable dealers upon whom he could have called for such a service. This request, it seemed to him, was fuelled by some desire for discretion, perhaps even secrecy.

– I get the impression, he replied at last, that Signor Grimaldi knows well his business. Would you like me to contact him on your behalf?

The writer assented to this, and they decided upon the following evening, if this were convenient for the signor. As he told Reuben the address he made one last request:

– Perhaps you would accompany him?

– Of course, Reuben replied.

Grimaldi quite jumped at the chance. Not because the enquirer was a famous writer (Reuben was not sure if Grimaldi even knew this), but because he was American and the merchant automatically, it seemed, associated wealth with a member of this nation. Grimaldi saw an opportunity in the invitation, and this was doubtless the reason he scolded Reuben when, that evening, the young man arrived late at his premises to collect him and go with him to the house in which the viewing was to take place. That afternoon, Reuben had got lost in his painted Venice, and time had quite slipped by. Reuben mumbled an incoherent excuse; he had no desire to inform Grimaldi that he was painting something other than family portraits.

– No one is currently in residence, the writer informed them when, on finding the address, they had knocked on the front door, only for it to be almost immediately opened to them.

The writer brought them into a small hallway and gestured for them to proceed into the front drawing room, which overlooked the *calle* and the small canal that ran parallel with it. There was an imposing fireplace in this room, but as the house had been uninhabited for some weeks there had been no fires lit, so he advised them to keep their coats on.

In the bay window, faintly revealed by the weak evening light still penetrating into the dark and sombre room, was the desk, the prime reason for Grimaldi's presence. To Reuben's untrained eye it had the appearance of a conventional davenport desk, and this judgement was confirmed when, glancing at Grimaldi's face, he read there the look of disappointment born of anticlimax, although he espied suddenly a secondary facial reaction: one of puzzlement on the dealer's part. Grimaldi actually looked directly at the writer as if to reproach him mutely for wasting his time with such a standard item of furniture. He then seemed to change his mind and returned his gaze to the object in question.

So, Grimaldi stood a while motionless, having a long look and nodding to himself. Then, before moving, he took the precaution to ask politely:

– May I touch it?

– Of course, of course, by all means. Please examine it. Let me get you some light.

They looked on as the writer retrieved an oil lamp, easily locating the container of matches on the mantel of the fireplace. Reuben offered to hold it for Grimaldi, and the writer assented. The illumination made for a quivering Vermeer interior, in which Reuben watched their features grow gaunter, cut across by blades of shade and shadow. The trio gathered around the desk. Up close, Reuben was more impressed by the ornate inlay on the desk's writing slope, which was in red leather with embossing and gilding.

Grimaldi unsnapped the clasp of the little leather bag he had been carrying and extracted a small, straight brush, not unlike a shaving one, only narrower and longer. Appraising the writing surface, he gently brushed the slope before lowering himself with a groan and a lot of creaking of knee joints. Thus able to bring his face close to the surface, he breathed on the leather as one would on a window or mirror. When the brief mist of his breath dispersed, he ran his fingers over the area and grunted to himself.

– It has been well used, he remembered to report to his observers standing behind him, but not damaged.

Using the desk to lean on, Grimaldi rose again and went around to its front. The pedestal structure of the desk was supported on two turned wooden feet with plainly carved supports; these supports were repeated under the writing slope. There were four drawers of different sizes with turned mahogany handles inserted into the right of the main pedestal. Giving a mute indication to these, he looked enquiringly at the writer.

– Please, you may examine as you see fit, he assured the dealer.

To Reuben, the drawers seemed to open and close smoothly on the runners. Grimaldi nodded to himself and also seemed satisfied with their operation. Next, he lifted the sloping surface and looked within. Then, checking behind him, he pulled a small study chair close and sat down, his examination of the item at an end. From this position he idly tapped the desk's surface while he looked at the writer over the rim of his spectacles, as if from a rampart or some vantage point, and Reuben read again that mixture of confusion and intrigue, and he thought the writer shifted slightly at his side, uneasy under such an intense scrutiny.

It seemed to act as a form of motivation for Grimaldi, for he rose quite suddenly and decided to inspect the object some more. He told Reuben to move around and tap the back panel with his knuckle. Exchanging a glance with the writer, Reuben went and knocked where he was told to, while Grimaldi raised once more the lid, leant into the desk and gave his ear to the interior.

– Ah, he said. Knock again, please.

This time, they all heard the hollow reverberation.

– It's a false back, the writer exclaimed.

– With a space between the inner and outer panels, Grimaldi added.

So saying, the dealer revisited the drawers, pulling them out of their sockets, until he stopped at the third one, for here he discovered a small sliding panel. Commanding Reuben to bring the lamp over, he pushed aside the panel to reveal a flat button. Reuben was aware of the writer drawing closer too, and when Grimaldi nodded decisively and reached in, the sharp stinging sound of the spring action release quite made them start. The sound reminded Reuben of an arrow hitting its target and vibrating loudly with the impact. All three of them gawped at the sudden revelation of a secret compartment hidden at the back of the drawer and the packet of papers it had been harbouring. Grimaldi actually stood up. Reuben could see the merchant's eyes glisten in the lustre of the oil lamp.

It suddenly felt to Reuben as if the temperature had risen in the room. Next, he realised that Grimaldi was staring at him; there was a deliberate and piercing intensity to the look he was exchanging with him. Indeed, the Italian appeared as if he were about to light upon the cache of letters, for such they appeared to Reuben to be in the lamp light, and dash off with them. He was trying to communicate some wordless appeal to him; he moved his head in a gesture that Reuben suddenly read as encouraging him to act as an accomplice. Startled, he shot a glance at the American; if he detected avarice in the features of one of the party, he read alarm in the face of the other.

This whirl of impressions was unfurling in mere seconds, but he had already understood that the furtive, secretive nature of these written correspondences seemed to have inflated their value, certainly in the eyes of the antiquarian. It came to him just as swiftly that they held greater emotional value for the writer, who, just then, as if once more reading his thoughts, also looked at him – or looked to him, he could not decide which. In the grim stillness that seemed to paralyse the three men, Reuben felt as much the intense centre of attention as the pile of papers; both of the other men were waiting to see whose side he would take.

There was then a sound from within the house. It might have been a floorboard creaking in the hallway or a riser on the staircase, the noise of the old house retracting in the cooler air of the evening; or, it immediately occurred to Reuben, there was another person present in the house. Whatever it was, the spell was broken; the tension dissipated and the writer seemed fortified enough to come forward and, reaching into the drawer, claim the bundle of letters.

– They are mine, he asserted, and when Grimaldi did not back off but appeared to continue to glare at the letters, he added, I mean, I wrote them; that is my handwriting. In an effort to lighten the mood further, he added: I write an abominable hand.

This confirmed for Reuben what had slowly been dawning on him: that they had belonged to the Lady, sent to her by the writer.

– But of course, Grimaldi was suddenly gracious and pleasant. And the desk?

– It remains for sale, the writer assured the dealer.

Minutes later, the deal sealed, as they were being escorted to the door, the writer had one last query:

– I imagine there is just the one secret drawer in a desk such as that?

– Just the one, Grimaldi confirmed.

At the corner of the street, as they were about to head their separate ways, Grimaldi observed:

– Those letters could have brought more money than the desk.

– I'm no expert, but I gather the money he accepted for it was something of a bargain, countered Reuben.

The dealer looked at him, and then, turning to go, said:

– It was repayment for finding those letters, for using my expertise. It is what I have realised Americans do: they make use of you. It is well that you are English.

– Irish, Reuben corrected, I am Irish.

– Same thing, the dealer said with a shrug.

– In the same way that you are Italian? Reuben said in mild provocation.

– Venetian, the older man retorted, and then: Oh, I see the point you are making. *Touché.*

He patted his young companion on the arm in a conciliatory fashion.

– I must go to my supper. My wife … he said vaguely.

Reuben stood and watched the merchant walk off into the now darker evening. Then, out of some vague pull of curiosity, instead of making his own way home he retraced his steps. Quite suddenly he pulled up sharply at the sight of the writer, overcoat collar up and hat pulled down tightly on his head, heading away from him up the street.

He might have called after the writer, only an unexpected sense of déjà vu gave him pause for thought. Something about the halting gait of the man, the bunching of his shoulders that Reuben could make out from his viewing position, recalled the similar figure he had spotted the previous day, on the periphery of the crowd that had gathered to watch the retrieval of the body from the canal.

It was then he smelt the smoke, and saw, on looking again, the flickers, as of flames issuing from the downstairs bay window of the house.

Sidling up to this, he peered in and was mystified to see the actual writer standing before a roaring fire, leaning on the mantel, one foot on the hearth, and all the time studying the recently revealed letters, one by one, by the illumination of the oil lamp and the grate. Reuben continued to watch as the writer, at intervals, having read each one, slowly, and it seemed with great sorrow, leaned forward and fed each letter to the blaze.

Part Two:
Ponte dei Sospiri

1.

The twin torchères, in the form of Moorish serving boys, looked almost lifelike to Reuben as he approached the palazzo on foot. As he drew near, other guests glided up magically to the wide sweep of water steps on the black swan of a gondola. Voices and laughter came down to him from the balconies and open windows above his head.

In the elaborately tiled entrance hall, Reuben presented the invitation that had arrived at his studio the previous afternoon. Knowing already that the palazzo belonged to a rich American woman, he suspected the writer's hand in the circumstance, but was excited nonetheless at the prospect of the little soirée.

He was shown up to a narrow, gallery-like salon on the first floor. At intervals, like sentries, French windows gave out onto the small balconies overhanging the Grand Canal. Cigar and cigarette smoke rolled in from outside and mingled pleasantly with the candle light that illuminated the salon as the building was not yet electrified. Reuben stood aside and, scrutinising long and hard, was not able to ascertain if the writer was one of the party of guests. They stood around in small groups conversing. His roving eye was arrested by the sight of a young woman swaying confidently through this company, and he straightened to attention at the sudden intuition that she was steering deliberately in his direction. She wore a dove-grey, almost sliver dress, which suited her narrow frame. Her hair was parted in the middle but fashioned into a tight chignon, which had the advantage of displaying her long, shapely neck. When she was older, he thought, a black velvet band would suit, but for the moment she appeared too young for such a provocation, even though he realised that he was himself a mere couple of years her elder.

– Mr Ross? she enquired. Are you not?

– I am, he assured her, although I fear you have me at a disadvantage. I know very few here, you see.

– Well, no matter. I am under strict instructions to talk to you.

– Really? Reuben replied. And to what purpose?

– Purpose? The young woman, girl really, pondered this before blithely returning: I suppose because you are a lot closer in age to me than the others. It's how, you see, I could tell you apart from this white and whiskery bunch.

– Thanks for that 'closer', he laughed. I'll take it as a compliment. And you are?

– Ursula, she replied. I'm from America.

– Are you indeed? said Reuben, at which she looked sharply at him.

– Are you making fun of me? she frankly enquired.

– A little, Reuben confessed. Your accent rather makes the claim for you. Have you been here long?

– Europe? she asked.

– Well … yes … Europe.

– Ages, she assured him. Then as an afterthought she added: if you say you know so few I will be able to point people out to you. Shall we?

So saying she took his arm and led him away from the entrance on into the *salle*.

– Well, he said to his new companion, you'll remember Venice I wager.

– Oh, Venice, she put it inconsequentially. It is very quiet. The absence of traffic I suppose.

And she proceeded to point out and identify the Bootes and Bronsons, Wisners and Curtises, and some Italian nobleman whose name she could not remember.

– The whole of Europe, a walrus-moustachioed man of military bearing was declaring, is little better than a standing camp numbering millions of armed men. Mark my words.

– That, Reuben's companion informed him, is the Marquess of Dufferin talking with Sir Dominick Ferrand. And that, she said, pausing and indicating a gentleman who was the centre of attention of a particularly large group, is Dr William Wilberforce Baldwin. I'm sure you have heard of *him*.

– I have, Reuben was relieved to be able to state. A physician to the community of wealthy expatriates.

– Everyone is intrigued by his presence here; he has recently arrived from Florence. People say he is here to treat a mystery patient. I think it is the King of Belgium, she confided in him.

– Despite the army of court physicians I suspect His Majesty may already have at his disposal? Reuben returned.

– Well, who do you think it is? she enquired sternly.

– Who, rather, is that lady? Reuben asked instead, having realised he was the sudden object of her pince-nez scrutiny. The girl turned around and immediately looked away again.

– Why did you make me look around? she scolded him. That is my aunt. I am travelling with her and she will not approve of me talking to a gentleman on my own. I must go.

Before Reuben could apologise, or suggest that she was hardly on her own, she had left his side and joined the group that included her aunt. Suddenly at a loss, he surveyed around and was startled to see the writer in the company all along, and more startled again to realise how nondescript he appeared, how somehow unassuming, standing on the edge of a group of grand-looking gentlemen, one of whom had just finished, to judge by the raucous laughter it seemed to merit, a bawdy joke or anecdote. The writer stole away at that point and came over to him, and Reuben realised that the writer had noted his presence well in advance of his own corresponding discovery.

– And what did you make of our most recent arrival from the New World? he immediately enquired.

– Recent? Reuben laughed at the statement. She informs me she has been here for 'ages'.

– If a fortnight qualifies as ages then she commits no falsehood.

– I don't think she found me very gallant: I was not able to defend her from the dragon.

– You mean of course my sister, the writer amusedly informed his companion. Ursula is my niece.

Reuben was struck dumb. In the face of this, the writer laughingly waved the statement away.

– Do not fret. I take no offence. And you're right: 'Come not between the dragon and its wrath.' Alicia disapproves of many of my friends and acquaintances. Your misfortune is that I recommend you, you see.

Reuben was still at the stammering stage when strains of music came to his rescue. Bewildered, he again looked around him for he had not been aware of there being musicians in the room. He then realised the notes were floating in with the purple haze through the windows and doors open to the night.

– Ah, the writer groaned, the incubi.

– I'm sorry?

– The night visitors. Come.

The writer took the young man by the arm and guided him out onto one of the small balconies. Looking down, they saw a fan-shape of gondolas, converged on the palazzo with a company of musicians dispersed among them. The building's lights glinted on the *ferros*[15] at the prows of the vessels and the bright lacquer of the polished wood. A gallery of beaming, illuminated faces were angled upwards towards them.

– They serenade the *padrona* of the house, the writer explained. She has become their benefactress you see, and when the evening trade has ended they oft-times assemble here to pay this homage.

– How is she their benefactress?

– When the tourists desert the city in winter, the writer explained, the gondoliers mostly fall on hard times. The *padrona* helps them out, financially or with food. For a lucky few she even renews their boats. Presently, she is on a mission to replace the neglected lamps that you see perched atop of or close by the *pali*[16] at the various *traghetti*, which are the boatmen's tutelary *Madonnetta*[17].

– And you disapprove? Reuben queried.

– Only of the music. It is quite atrocious.

Despite this observation, they remained looking down on the colourful spectacle until at length the recital ended and, with extravagant bows and doffing of hats, the gondoliers dispersed and went off in different directions. In the comparative silence that ensued, the writer lit a cigarette and blew contemplative plumes out over the canal. Eventually he appeared to arrive at a decision, and turning to his companion enquired of him a second time what he had thought of the young American.

– She was very pleasant company, Reuben assured him.

The writer nodded in acceptance of this statement, and his seeming to mull it over prompted Reuben to ask why it was so important to him what he thought.

– Because, he at length replied, I was thinking that she would be perfect to wear the gown. For the picture.

– I see, Reuben replied, with enough hesitation to prompt an enquiring look from the writer.

– I already had someone in mind, Reuben explained.

– A foreigner? the writer retorted. Italian?

– Well, yes. Would that be a problem? Reuben returned, not a little taken aback.

Instead of answering immediately, the writer turned away from the view of the glimmering canal and, leaning back against the balustrade, regarded instead the inner scene.

– It's a matter of the real thing, he attempted to explain. My niece, you see, is the real thing.

– Meaning American, Reuben countered.

The writer did not engage with this assertion; instead, he declared:

– Well, let us not decide now. Let us sleep on it, as they say.

There was a tone in this last that indicated their conversation was at its end. The writer tossed the remainder of his cigarette over the edge of the balcony and went off to rejoin the other guests. Reuben somehow knew he was not meant to follow him this time.

Back in the spacious entrance hall, with a footman off to retrieve his overcoat, it suddenly struck him that he had not been formally introduced to the rich American hostess. And he feared rather for the rude health of his commission, feeling as he did that he had incurred the writer's displeasure.

2.

It was only when he was outside again, and strolling along a smaller, arterial ria, that he realised a gauze of sea-fret had rolled in off the laguna, drawing buildings and objects more intimately close. Yet despite this dim blindfold of fog, he was able to make out the lamp-glow of one of the shrines the writer had so recently been describing to him. Pausing to study the illuminated statue, Reuben suddenly jolted upright with fright as a voice out of nowhere said:

– We have a mutual friend.

A man stepped out of the mist and was suddenly standing there at his side.

– I'm sorry? Reuben stammered, looking down at this apparition.

– I saw you together just now on the balcony, the man explained.

In the dim, sacramental light, Reuben scrutinised his interlocutor. He noted a dark patina of damp on the shoulders of his overcoat, the exposed buttons of which reflected the lamplight; little beads of moisture glinted on the brim of his round hat of hard black felt.

– You were at the soirée? Reuben asked.

– Alas, no. I saw you from without. I have seen you before though, he assured Reuben, although his statement seemed to be accompanied by an arched eyebrow that momentarily disappeared up under the brim of his hat.

– At Mme Merimée's, the man continued, although we did not make each other's acquaintance.

– No. Indeed. We would not have. Reuben was immediately curt with the man and turned to be on his way.

– Please, may I accompany you a bit of the way? My pensione is in this direction I believe, and what with this mist and all….

Without awaiting Reuben's assent, the man fell into step beside him.

– My name is John Drake, he decided to inform his new companion, telling him also the name of his pensione.

Reuben merely nodded, but gave no objection to the man's presence. He had recognised the establishment mentioned and knew its location to be in the general direction they were taking, somewhere ahead of them in the thickening fog. But Drake was not to be silent.

– You are friends with the great man? he returned to his subject.

– You can tell that from outside?

– Well, yes, I suppose. But I've also done my enquiries. You see, I professionally occupy myself with other people's business. It's my business if you like, he declared proudly.

This statement halted Reuben in his tracks.

– You're a newspaper man, he exclaimed.

– A journalist, John Drake amended. European corre-spondent for a most respectable organ: *The Register*.

– I have not read it, Reuben informed the reporter, and restarted his walk.

– I merely endeavour to obtain material for a particularly, if I may say so, discerning London readership. Drake was obviously at pains to convince Reuben.

Reuben remained silent, but the man seemed to take this as a licence to obtain some such material, for he plainly said:

– There have been rumours surrounding the recent death of a lady friend of his here in Venice.

This drew Reuben up a second time, and he turned on his interlocutor.

– Rumours? he snapped.

– She fell to her death.

Drake whispered this last, while at the same time peering behind him. This action made Reuben do likewise, and he realised that what had at first been spiralling threads of mist were gradually braiding and combining to coalesce as thick, viscous fog that was threatening to envelop the two men. Returning his gaze to his unwelcome companion, Reuben shook his head in dismissive fashion and walked on, remarking only:

– She was, I believe, delirious with fever.

The man quickened his pace to catch up with Reuben.

– Do you know they shared a villa in Florence?

– I did not, Reuben gave as terse reply.

– All very respectable, I hasten to add. They occupied separate wings. They were very discreet. I checked. I've spoken with the servants.

– It does not sound like a very interesting story then, Reuben remarked.

– Oh but it does, Drake insisted. The lack of a story might just *be* the story.

– The lack of a story? quizzed Reuben

– Scandal, then, Drake restated it. The lack of scandal just might be the thing.

He had no sooner made this declaration than he suddenly stopped. There was something infectious about the man's overcautious anxiety, and Reuben felt the need to peer about him again. Drake was gathering the collar of his coat together against the damp clamminess of the murk.

– I do so miss the sound of traffic, he lamented, and the smell of horses.

– I thought you'd be used to fog, Reuben replied. What did Oscar Wilde say? 'London is all sad people and fogs. I don't know whether fogs produce the sad people, or the sad people produce the fogs.'

Ignoring the quip, but becoming more animated, Drake asked:

– Do you know Oscar Wilde? And when Reuben laughed at the enquiry, added lamely: you are Irish after all.

Walking on, Reuben informed the reporter that, as best he could tell, they were near his lodgings.

– Our friend and he do not get on, you know, Drake confided. You should hear some of the things they say about one another that are reported to me.

Reuben remained non-committal, which only prompted Drake to continue:

– And yet he supported Wilde's unsuccessful candidacy for membership of the Saville Club.

– I'm afraid that I don't have the honour of frequenting such establishments. I believe you turn here for your lodgings.

Drake peered warily at the *ramo*[18] indicated; it seemed to be swallowed by a low *sottoportico*[19], which they could just make out yawning at them through the fog.

– You need publicity then, Drake thought to counsel him. Do not underestimate the benefits that would accrue from a felicitous mention in my forthcoming letter from Venice.

While Reuben stood pondering this last statement, he was caught rather off guard by the blunt enquiry that followed it.

– Are you doing a painting of the great man?

– A sketch, he stammered. Nothing big or important. I really must be on my way.

– There is a passable café close to my pensione. Please, meet me there tomorrow around eleven. We can discuss some more.

Reuben looked down to find that a business card had unaccountably appeared in his hand. He looked up, but the voice had become a disembodied one as the man had merged now with the swirling mist, disappearing, it struck him, with the same alacrity of his entrance.

As Reuben proceeded into the Canareggio district, in his head he seemed to stumble blindly through its own fog of confusion, chasing a half-formed thought that tantalisingly evaded his mind's grasp, born out of the obscure, almost mischievous, mention of Florence. It was only as he approached his own dwelling that the idea suddenly loomed clear for him. It was not the possibility of matrimony that prompted the reporter's prying into the writer's relationship with the Lady of the laguna. It was rather, Reuben suddenly realised, the impossibility of it that excited so the little man from London.

3.

The writer's fulminating missive came the next morning, warning Reuben that *a denizen of the fourth estate is prowling the precincts of Venice.*

It is a ghastly newspaperised world we inhabit, the letter lamented. *By far the most striking sign of our age, I fear, is this inexplicable mania for publicity.*

Reuben stood in the middle of the studio, conflicted. In one hand he held the letter; in the other Drake's calling card. He looked again at the letter, the words gouged into the paper by a violent nib. They inveighed against *the invasion, the impudence and shamelessness of the newspaper and the extinction of all sense between public and private.*

Reuben went to the window and considered the mist, which still persisted outside. The letter's last line read: *I know I can depend, my dear friend, on your discretion.*

Reuben's father could only offer so much financial support, and even this was put in some doubt with the news in his most recent letters from home of increased political unrest between the landowners and their tenants. According to his father, Reuben's old friend Thomas

Lynch was becoming very active in the county, stoking such unrest. *Bordering on the seditious* had been one of his father's phrases. It all made Drake's intimation of publicity, and the remuneration that might accrue, very enticing.

At first he wondered if there were some other newsworthy item unrelated to the writer with which to satiate the journalist, but he only really knew Dalglish, who was struggling as much as himself. There was the Norwegian painter, perhaps, but again, outside a small circle of young artists, he was as little known as Reuben, and therefore could be of no currency to Drake or of interest to his discerning London readership.

What then if he were to give Drake a glowing portrait of the writer, supplying nothing but flattering details: the generosity extended to the likes of himself, the man's erudition and insights, his guidance and advice, his humour? Would these snippets not satisfy the newspaperman? he deluded himself into surmising.

In the end, he determined to go and test the limits of Drake's inquisitiveness to see if he could honourably accommodate whatever it was Drake sought without compromising the writer or damaging his own association with the great man.

In this frame of mind, he folded the letter and put it into the inside pocket of his overcoat. Then he searched around for his hat.

The place of rendezvous was really a waterside drinking shop; great tarry barges were drawn up nearby. A large gallows-like derrick unloaded barrels onto the wharf. Inside the establishment, he looked in vain for the journalist. He could not see him, although it was the appointed hour. Finding a seat, he surveyed around him and judged any coffee on sale to be unmentionable, the wine undesignated, tea non-existent. He opted, therefore, for a mug of cloudy beer, which he nursed until it was almost forty-five minutes after the hour. Then he left the unfinished beer and the unprepossessing premises and stepped out again into the enduring mist.

He had intended to make his way home, but the sight of a woman sweeping the steps of the pensione that Drake had named the night before prompted him to approach her and make enquiries. The woman looked at him with some alarm.

– Are you a friend of the signore?

– I had an appointment with him, he explained.

– Signore Drake has left Venice.

– Oh, Reuben replied.

– He was attacked, you see. Last night, she added.

– Good God, Reuben exclaimed.

– *Si*. Just there.

Reuben looked in the direction she was pointing, though with the mist the precise location was merely notional. However, the apparent proximity of the incident in both time and place to where he had parted company with the newspaperman alarmed him.

– Was he hurt? he asked, turning back to the lady.

– The shoulder of his frock-coat is torn. And my husband finds his hat this morning.

At this moment, the door to the establishment that Reuben had just vacated opened, and raucous laughter accompanied by a thumping of tables erupted outdoors, and the landlady rolled her eyes to heaven and shrugged her shoulders as if suggesting a suspected source of the trouble that had befallen the Englishman.

– He has left Venice, she repeated with a heavy sigh.

As Reuben walked away, however, tipping his hat, he began to recall the numerous times the journalist had checked behind him, as if looking out for something or someone. He passed through the *sottoportico*, which appeared to him even more carnivorous than it had done the night before. Once through it he stopped himself and surveyed around him, although expecting to see what he did not know. Then, as nothing of any particular note caught his attention, he proceeded on his way.

Part Three:
Ponte del Tette

1.

The next day, the mist remained, plugging the channels, rias and canal-ways, and there was no contact from the writer. The day after that, the gondoliers went on strike.

A small fleet of vessels, *sandoli*[20] and gondolas, blockaded the headquarters of the *Societa Vaporetti Omnibus di Venezia*, including, menacingly, a hunting skiff with the long-barrelled *spingarda*[21] poking over its prow. Tito informed him that their plaints were not just due to loss of trade, but loss of life too. Recent fatalities were being put down to the swells and surges caused by the passage of the steamers; smaller vessels had been overturned or people toppled overboard. One victim had been caught up in the screws of the bigger vessel.

The strike would last for three days, by the end of which they would come to an agreement with the mayor. He was never going to abolish completely the 'little steamers'; they were, he saw, the future, and Venice could not stand still. However, he did agree to limit the number of stops the steam launches could make and to restrict them to the Canallazo and the hours of daylight. The little intricate clockwork of smaller canals and shadowy waterways would remain the remit of the gondoliers.

To Reuben, it all amounted to having no great expectation of contact that first day. Yet, just before the middle of the day, his landlady ascended to his studio shaking vigorously the writer's calling card in her hand.

– *Avanti!* Reuben heartily hailed the writer from the head of the stairs.

Blowing hard, and a little red in the face, the writer appeared, a large parcel under his arm. No mention was made of the journalist, for on entering the studio the writer's eyes were drawn immediately to the Venice-scape, the product of the day spent out on the laguna prior to that first sighting of the writer. Reuben had been touching at it on the easel that very morning.

– I'm afraid the light's not very good today, Reuben said ruefully.

The writer bent down and deposited the parcel on the floor, then he scrutinised long and hard the work in progress, moving in close one minute, withdrawing a few steps the next, crossing and uncrossing his arms, cocking his head first one way then the other, then simply standing with his hands behind his back.

– It has been done *sur le motif*? he enquired without turning to address him directly.

– Well, *en plein air*, yes, Reuben half-whispered in return.

Eventually, his visitor picked up the parcel again and turned to him with a smile and a judgement:

– It is extraordinarily immediate. But I think Mr Ruskin would accuse you of pitching the paint pot at the canvas.

Marvelling inwardly at how relieved he was with what he took to be the writer's approbation, Reuben related how this was the painting executed the day of the laguna.

– Ah, the writer responded, and he appraised anew the composition as if checking to see if his own image was somewhere recorded amidst the swirls and arabesques of colour.

– Speaking of which, I've come about my request, he mentioned over his shoulder.

– Is that perhaps … the gown? Reuben suggested more than enquired.

– It is, the writer affirmed. I've arrived at the decision to proceed, and furthermore to do so with your choice of model.

The artist nodded gravely in the face of this declaration. Recalling the writer's reaction on the balcony on the night of the soirée, Reuben was intrigued by this volte-face.

– And your niece?

– Perhaps she is not the real thing after all. I may have been mistaken.

He said no more, his vanity perhaps rendering him disinclined to discuss mistakes or misapprehensions. However, the look he gave Reuben seemed to tell the tale: the young lady had evidently not passed the test; she had not proven to be 'susceptible'. In his mind's eye he imagined her horrified, or perhaps simply bored, reaction to the painting as she shuddered in the dank interior of the church. He almost smiled at the scenario.

– In any case, the writer was continuing, I only require an esquisse. It's merely a memento, no full-blown portrait.

– Of course.

– You may keep the features vague; *flou*[22], as it were.

Reuben nodded his assent and looked pointedly in the direction of the bulky parcel that the writer still clasped to him. Then his ears pricked up at the familiar footfall on the landing that announced for him Gina's arrival.

– *Scusi*! she exclaimed on appearing and realising he was entertaining a guest.

The two men turned and regarded Gina, who had stopped suddenly on the threshold, centred in the doorframe, wearing a velvet jacket and black kid gloves, each with one little white button. If anything, the writer seemed to tighten his grip on the package so that Reuben quickly made the introductions and Gina, sensing the stature of this potential client, gave a pretty and respectful curtsy to the guest, who greeted her in fluent and unaccented Italian.

– Perhaps, Reuben suggested, we may see now the gown?

Reluctantly, the writer looked around him for a clean and uncluttered surface. Seeing this, Reuben hastened to clear and wipe a tabletop, and the writer undid the packaging and shook out the gown for all to see. Length-wise it would fit Gino, but in English, doubtless out of a sense of delicacy and decorum, and fishing around for the right form of words, the writer addressed Reuben:

– I fear, however, that the embonpoint may be….

And suddenly his face fully reddened as his eyes fell on one of Reuben's nudes recumbent, the unframed canvas leaning up against the far wall, and in which the writer recognised the model whose small, pert breasts were in full view for his appraisal.

– *Cossa ha ditto*? demanded Gina.

– *Niente*, Reuben laughingly assured her. Then:

– Gina is a skilled seamstress and will find a solution, he assured the writer.

– Of course, the writer stammered, and in part to cover his discomfort declared: there is also this.

He revealed a book that had also been part of the parcel. Handing it to Reuben, he asked him if he was acquainted with the text or author. Reuben examined the spine and raised his eyebrows on reading: *The Law of Psychic Phenomena* by a Thomas Jay Hudson. Looking at the writer, he shook his head.

– The underlinings you will see of some passages are hers, the writer explained, not mine. I find the propositions quite preposterous, but I thought it would give you some insight, as it were, to inform the drawing. When will you start?

All the time his eyes followed Gina, who had gently taken the gown from him and was examining it over by the large window. She announced to them that some alterations would be needed and a starting date in two days' time was agreed. As the writer readied himself to depart, Reuben asked him if he had come on foot.

– I *can* walk, the writer countered. I'm not so decrepit! On terra firma, I can assure you, I am a keen cyclist. When in London, I fence.

– Well then, allow me to accompany you part of the way, Reuben requested, pocketing the volume and looking around for his hat.

Having agreed to Reuben's offer, once outside they nevertheless strolled along for some time in silence. It was as if relinquishing the last gown had plunged the writer into deep reflection, and it was only when they came at last onto the esplanade of the Riva degli Schiavoni, with the view of the far lagoon suggesting itself through the mist, which was beginning to thin itself to the consistency of what the Venetians referred to as a '*caligo*', that spirits revived and the power of speech returned. Stopping to gaze out at the faint sheen of water, he said:

– Her exquisite influence quite sinks into your spirit. She is always interesting and almost always sad; she has a thousand occasional graces and is always liable to happy accidents.

Reuben listened in polite silence by his side, and when at length he gauged that the writer was to say no more, took the liberty to enquire:

– Of whom do you speak, sir?

– Of whom? Why I speak of Venice of course, who else? *La Serenissima*[23]. It is quite the easiest place in the world, you see, to personify.

They had halted now at the point of going their separate ways, the writer's residence some doors away, and yet Reuben wanted to linger for longer in his company.

– At least, he remarked with relief, the fog looks like lifting. And not before time, if you ask me.

– Ah, the writer returned, but I'm quite for the fog; contrary, I appreciate, to what appears to be the common taste. Hawthorne, for example, referred to fog as 'the ghost of mud, the spiritualised medium of departed mud.' For many fog is an impression; for me it is an experience. One feels enclosed, contained in one's own private world.

– Do you shun so the public world?

The writer shrugged his wide shoulders.

– It can be a vulgar and unaccommodating place.

He exchanged a long look with Reuben on this, and then, nodding, went off in the direction of his abode.

Reuben's way took him to a drinking house.

The English and the American tourists like to take their shade on hot days. The Italian workers also like to take an *ombre*, but this describes a late afternoon early evening drink, a reward for that day's labour. On his way back to the studio, Reuben decided to take one himself, stopping in a local *birreria* where he ordered a drink and a small plate of *sarde in saór*. Sitting by the window, he sipped his beer, and remembering the book took it out and began to leaf through it, dwelling on certain passages as they caught his attention. He finished his first beer and ordered a second.

Reuben felt a natural inclination to dismiss in sardonic fashion the author's odd theories. When, for example, Hudson invited the reader to ponder why most apparitions are *always well provided with apparel*, he tried in vain to suppress laughter, which drew the attention of his fellow drinkers. *Ghosts don't like being naked either*, he thought, recalling the early, awkward love sessions with Gina. Returning to the text, the author's explanation was simple: the soul of the dead put on the soul of the clothes. 'We must therefore suppose,' the author argued, 'that clothes, however improbably, have souls.'

The late afternoon had darkened into early evening, and the barman lit some oil lamps suspended from the low-raftered ceiling. Turning in his seat so that some of the weak illumination fell on the page, he read Hudson's belief that phantoms were 'embodied thought'. He wrote of ghosts being a form of telepathic communication, in particular where emotions and events were of an intense nature as, the writer suggested, in cases of death by violence. This psychic energy could somehow imprint itself into walls, furniture and belongings, and so, it seemed, accounted for hauntings.

Then Reuben was squinting, and it was too dark to see clearly the print, including the margin notes that he knew to be in the Lady's hand. He settled the bill and went home.

While adamant that the book's theories amounted to hocus pocus garnished with pseudo-scientific language, he was still mulling them over when, on climbing the stairs and swinging open the door to his studio, he emitted an involuntary cry at the frightful sight of the grey gown looming up before him in the twilight, floating in mid-air. Having heard his terrified shriek, the landlady appeared behind him with a light, and they both found themselves gazing at the gown, suspended on a coat hanger from a hook in the ceiling. Gina had evidently put it there to allow the creases to fall from the thick grey material.

Embarrassed, Reuben apologised and attempted to laugh off the incident. Sniffing the beer on his breath, the landlady gave a disapproving look and turned away.

2.

There was something of the theatre of the *commedia dell'arte all'improvviso* about Lynch's arrival in Venice.

Reuben was standing on the platform at the precise time Lynch's letter told him the train from Paris would arrive, and on seeing Lynch detrain from one of the far carriages he waved with the gusto that seeing an old boyhood friend for the first time since he had gone abroad merited. Yet Lynch did not respond in like manner, and at first Reuben put this down to the man-made fog of steam and smoke emitting from the locomotive and which briefly enwrapped the passengers, obscuring their vision; black flakes of soot and cinder blew about too. However, when Lynch proceeded to stride purposefully along the platform towards him, then level with him, and then past him, without hesitation or acknowledgement, as though he were an invisible man, Reuben's stomach churned as he began to understand the purpose of this performance. Lynch, he realised, had picked up a shadow, and to protect himself Reuben continued to pantomime an enthusiastic waving motion at what was now some non-existent imaginary traveller still disembarking.

Mindful of the warnings in the letters from his father, Reuben turned after what he judged to be a prudent length of time and surveyed the backs of the recently arrived, but could not make out who might be trailing Lynch.

He was about to follow the returnees and arrivals when something about his immediate surroundings stalled him. There was an ear-piercing screech from the engine, an asthmatic release of steam, the clang of metal, and something else he realised he had not heard for a while: the dissonant roar of porters and officials having to raise the level of their voices above the mechanical and clamorous sounds of the railway station. Away from the drip of water and the dazzle of reflection, he felt he could be once more in any of the great cities of Europe, and as he breathed in the vapours of oil and coal fumes they seemed to speak to him of the world outside the island city, and the sudden urge was on him to place a boot on one of the lower rungs and hoist himself on board the train, though it was not due to pull out from Venice until the evening.

When he emerged eventually, and regarded once more the bridges and canals, they took on the fantastical appearance of manufactured sets and scenery, constructed and designed for some great operatic pageant and performance. He looked to see if he could spot Lynch, but he had already melted into the labyrinth of the city. On a whim, he glanced around him lest he were also the subject of some surveillance, but seeing no one pay him any particular attention he decided to return to the studio and wait there for Lynch to make contact.

It was not a long wait. That afternoon, Dalglish, the engraver from Glasgow, called to take him to his workshop, where Lynch was waiting.

Reuben had met Dalglish through the small social grouping of impecunious expatriate artisans who frequented the cheaper hostelries in the city. In truth, the Scotsman had gravitated towards him on hearing he came from Ireland. Although, on occasions, he had hinted at some political involvement with what he termed 'the Irish cause' – pamphleteering, attending meetings, fundraising – Dalglish only now revealed a closer connection he had forged with the Irish Republican Brotherhood in Glasgow. Reuben felt a little piqued at the thought that Lynch had arrived in Venice with more than his own name as a potential contact. Lynch had evidently had little difficulty getting in touch with the Scot.

The workshop was dimly lit and reeked of glue and the stench of sulphur. When they entered, Lynch got up quickly from his seat and came forward with his hand extended.

– Robert, he said. It's been a while.

– You look well, Thomas, Reuben replied, accepting the warm handshake.

Dalglish had whisky to offer them, and while he was away getting it the two friends settled down around the work table strewn with the tools of the engraver's trade.

– My father informs me you are a *hillsider* now, Reuben said. A Fenian. I take it that explains the intrigue at the train station?

Lynch sat back and laughed.

– I must apologise for the subterfuge, he said.

Then, in a more serious tone, he sat forward and stated:

– There is a secret police, you know.

– Where? Reuben asked, alarmed.

Lynch smiled in a rueful fashion and replied:

– I'm bound to say everywhere, but that would make me sound quite high-strung, would it not; a little alarmist?

Reuben shrugged and said nothing.

– In Scotland Yard, Lynch continued. A special branch to hunt us down.

– Us?

– The growing number of us who have had enough of beards and pince-nez politics, Lynch retorted. The halfway house of the Home Rulers.

And Lynch proceeded to tell Reuben about the state of things with Parnell gone; many of the young activists were no longer impressed by constitutional politics, especially in light of the bitter divisions between the pro- and anti-Parnellites in the Home Rule Party.

– Parnell was growing cold towards the farmer cause anyway, bored with peasant proprietorship. Sure, didn't he visit Belfast? He was getting too cosy with the industrialists and the Protestants.

– So you want to start the Land War again, the return of Captain Moonlight? Reuben interjected. Remember how your father used to tell us in the schoolhouse about the debacle of '68?

– We must learn from that failure, Lynch replied. And we must learn from Europe. Revolutionary ferment is all over the Continent, and I have been sent to study it, to make contacts, and perhaps raise some funds along the way.

– I'm afraid, said Reuben hastily, I cannot help you there. I don't know anyone of any influence in Venice.

– I have come merely to catch up with an old friend, Lynch laughed Reuben's concern away, though added: the only favour I would ask of you would be to consider returning home in the near future to help your father.

Reuben stared at Lynch.

– Help him? He is not unwell, Reuben countered. I am in regular contact. Has he sent you to say this?

Lynch shook his head and sat forward to explain himself better.

– Your father has always been a landowner with moderate views, sympathetic to the tenants.

– He has always supported land reform, Reuben concurred.

– However, Lynch added, he is getting old. Mairead Reilly still works as a maid for him, and tells us he no longer has the energy or will to raise his voice in support of change.

Reuben's face coloured slightly at the mention of the maid's name, but in the half-light it seemed to go unnoticed.

– She says, Lynch pointedly continued, he often talks of you.

– And you think I should return to add my voice to his? I am neither a politician nor a farmer, Reuben insisted. I paint. I live here now.

Lynch sat back and drained his glass of whisky. Then, looking squarely at Reuben, he asked:

– Where is your country?

– Ireland. I have little choice: my country is Ireland, Reuben declared.

Lynch nodded, and after a moment of contemplation he got up from his seat.

– I leave Venice tonight. The moonlight flit, you might say. I have things to do before departure.

Reuben rose as well then and accepted Lynch's farewell handshake. Dalglish went to look out the front window of the workshop to see if the coast was clear. Waiting, Lynch took the opportunity to inform Reuben further:

– There is more than rural discontent happening at home. There is a wave of new nationalism, a conviction among many that we should be separate.

Reuben stared at Lynch, but hung fire.

– Your father could do with you being at his side. Supporting him.

– Protecting him? Reuben sought clarity.

Lynch shrugged his shoulders.

– Who knows what is going to happen? he replied.

When Dalglish told them he could see no one suspicious watching the premises, Reuben curtly nodded and went out.

3.

Tito was helping Reuben stretch a canvas when the two *carabinieri*[24] called, and so was able to communicate to the momentarily flustered Reuben that they wanted him to accompany them to a local *gendarmeria* to answer a few enquiries.

– What enquiries? Reuben asked, turning to the two *militi*.

One of the officers rattled some words off in reply.

– They will not say, Tito informed the artist. Don't worry; I will get help.

The two officers brought Reuben to a nondescript building not far from where Signor Grimaldi's shop was located. On the way, they merely shrugged their shoulders or indicated that they did not understand his use of Italian, by way of deflecting the anxious questions he posed them, until finally he too lapsed into a reflective silence. Coming so swiftly after the event, he could only assume that this attention was due to the clandestine meeting with Lynch. At one point along the way, however, he was heartened by the thought that it may well have to do with the recent attack on the journalist Drake.

The room he was led into was bare and unaccommodating but for the basic furnishings of chairs and a table at
which sat a thickset man who did not look up or in any way
react to their entrance. On one wall hung a crucifix, while on
another dangled, in heart shape, a pair of wrought-iron hand
manacles. Reuben was no connoisseur of pipe tobacco, but
the smog of shag smoke that filled the room reminded him
of the smell of London and informed him that the thickset
man was probably from that city too. The man's pale com-
plexion and florid cheeks increased the impression that he
was not Italian: the cockney accent confirmed it.

– Have a seat, he said to Reuben, indicating the one
situated opposite where he was positioned behind the desk.

With a grunt, he dismissed the two Italian officers.

– They don't speak much English, he complained to
Reuben.

– No, Reuben commiserated. It's quite inconvenient.

The burly man looked up sharply at this.

– May I ask what this is about? Reuben hastily enquired.

– What it's about?! the man snapped back. It's about
anarchists and insurgency. It's about threats to the state. It's
about this man.

Somewhat startled by the sharp, staccato delivery
of the man, Reuben looked aghast as the man pushed a
daguerreotype across the surface of the desk for him to
study. It was not of great quality, but Reuben could make
out that it was Lynch.

– We've been following him since he left Ireland. He's been to London, then Paris.

Reuben found himself nodding at this information. He looked up at the man.

– And now he's here in Venice, the man informed him. Which is where you come in. You've met with him, have you not?

Reuben's heart hammered so loudly in his chest he feared the man could hear it; he found it hard to breathe.

– May I ask who you are? He decided to buy some time with this enquiry.

– I work for Superintendent William Melville of Scotland Yard. I'm sure you've heard of him, him being a fellow Irishman and all. He's good at tracking down Fenians.

All the time listening, Reuben could make out that the man had a file of papers before him, from which he had extracted the photograph of Lynch. Assuming that he was therefore well informed, Reuben pointed to the photograph and stated:

– I've known him from childhood; his father was the local schoolmaster.

– And you've met up with him here.

His interrogator was stating this, not suggesting it, although there was something of a bluff in the tone of voice. The detective was guessing that a meeting had already taken place, and Reuben quickly reasoned that the best line to take was to confirm that this was so. He had, he hoped to demonstrate, nothing to hide.

– Only for old time's sake. I am no anarchist, sir.

The man merely grunted in response to this and pushed a blank sheet of paper and a pen across the desk to Reuben.

– Write there the location at which you met him and where we might find him now.

Thinking about Dalglish, Reuben said:

– We met yesterday afternoon at a *bacàro*.

– A what?

– A sort of public house. He said he was leaving Venice last night.

– He did not do so by train. We had agents waiting. Write the address of this 'backarow' place.

Reuben lifted the pen, and without hesitation wrote down the directions to the drinking shop that Drake had suggested for the rendezvous that had failed to take place. He adjudged it to be a rough enough establishment for the clientele not to give information to officers of the law too willingly.

Taking the paper and scrutinising it for a moment, the man pushed himself back in the chair and got to his feet. He was suddenly looming over Reuben.

– I'll go and show this to my Italian colleagues, he informed Reuben. I will ask you to sit here quietly. I might be gone some time.

– You can't just keep me here, Reuben protested. I have work to do. I'm an artist with commissions to finish.

– You'll stay here as long as I want, the detective growled. And if I find out you've been telling me untruths, you'll see then how long I can keep you here as our guest.

The man lifted the file of documents, including the sheet of paper on which Reuben had written, and left the room. Reuben looked around with some alarm at the sound of a key turning to lock the door. Sitting there and finding the room suddenly hot and stifling, Reuben got up and went to the window and opened it to let out some of the pipe smoke. It overlooked a small back yard surrounded by a high wall. In the middle of the yard was an overturned gondola sitting on saw horses, exposing a bottom punctured with gaping holes.

He returned to his seat to wait, taking out and peering at his timepiece.

It was almost on the hour mark that he suddenly sat up in the seat and turned in the direction of the locked door. Frowning, he got to his feet, prompted to do so by the conviction that someone was standing on the other side.

– Is there someone there? he enquired, first in English, followed by Italian.

All he got by way of response was a heavy silence.

– You can't keep me here, he announced in a bolder, more determined voice. I am not a prisoner.

There was still no reply, but also no lessening of the impression that someone was in the corridor. Reuben raised his fist to resound his discontent on the door, when a chilly stillness stalled his hand. Instead, he brought his ear close to the door. For moments he remained in this attitude, hardly breathing, trying to discern who was without. Perhaps as a result of the open window, the temperature seemed to have suddenly dropped in the room.

Then he was startled by the sound of a distant door opening and heavy footsteps coming down the corridor. They stopped outside the office. Reuben stepped swiftly away from the door, which was now being unlocked. It swung open to reveal the English detective in the doorway flanked by a *carabiniere*. The detective waved another piece of paper in his hand.

– Well, he sneered, advancing into the room and causing Reuben to take some more steps back, it seems you are possessed of friends with a bit of influence. Who'd have thought it?

– I'm free to go? Reuben asked.

– Your Yankee friend assures us that you are a respectable law-abiding citizen. It seems we're to let you go. But don't think we're not watching.

Abashed, Reuben looked around for his hat, and retrieving it made for the door, only to be delayed by the cautionary tone of the detective's parting shot:

– The Americans will do you no good in the long run, you know. They're only ever out for themselves.

Reuben did not reply. Instead, he stepped into the corridor and looked up and down it, but there was only himself and the *carabiniere* there. He could see no one else.

4.

The day of the drawing dawned with a freshening wind blowing down from the Dolomites and across the Veneto Plain. It blew over the wetlands and the sand flats; it fretted the huge *bilance da pesca* fishing nets webbing the estuaries. It stirred herons and egrets into watchful flight above the canna reeds. It blew along the Piave River and the Tagliamento River and into the city itself, siphoning through large and little canals alike, causing wave-slap and clothes flap and craft to see-saw on the water. It blew through the window shuffling loose leaves and sketches and making sway the grey material of the hanging dress, lifting its hem. Outside again, it blew away any tattered memory of mist, and the studio flooded with crisp and salty sea-light.

A *fiasco* of Friulian wine sat on the table by the window as Reuben expected the writer to attend the commencement of the composition. He had purchased it in his local *bacàro*. In the event, the writer requested tea.

As he prepared it, Reuben said:

– Were you afraid I would break my neck trying to escape across the rooftops like Casanova?

However, his tentative allusion to the letter the English detective had received was greeted with a baffled stare from the writer, and Reuben hastily apologised the comment away by saying it was a silly nonsensical joke.

The artist sat him in a ladder-back chair slightly to the side and out of his own line of sight. Then they both looked up as the creak of the floorboards announced Gina's emerging from the sleeping quarters where she had changed into the gown. The writer was suddenly on his feet again.

With her hair caught up in a chignon, she smiled awkwardly at the two spectators, one of whom looked as if he did not recognise her at all, while the other looked as if he almost did, for Reuben registered the mixture of shock and admiration that suddenly played across the writer's face as he beheld the model. As for himself, he was struck by the transformational effect the garment had on his model: she seemed to float towards them, modest yet elegant, no longer the boisterous, outgoing girl to whom he had become accustomed. Both men almost bowed in acknowledgement of her sudden appearance.

She went and took up a standing position where a small cross had been chalked on the studio floor, like an actor's stage mark. Standing, they had agreed, would show the gown off to fullest effect, especially as Gina had noticed a subtle opaline hue hidden in the depths of the material, which only came to light under the close scrutiny that accompanied her alterations. The sun's highlighting of the dress confirmed Gina's discovery, and Reuben was already mixing in his mind the colours that would capture it for him; already he was lost in the work, his materials lined up on the work surface by his easel. Quietly, he became oblivious to Gina and the writer, and to the tramontana that continued to blow outside. There was now only the feel of the brush going into the colour and then onto the canvas; only the figure, that vague, elegant form he was endeavouring to capture.

So he had no way of gauging the time, of knowing how long he had been engrossed, before some subtle change in the general make-up, mood and composition made him conscious of having missed something in the room. Perhaps it was the enlargement of his model's eyes that alerted him to the look of concern that suddenly darkened her features. He frowned, a little angry at being distracted from the task in hand, as if her stance or bearing needed to be adjusted. With his brush in mid-air, he straightened up from behind the easel to better judge, and seeing him raise his head enquiringly she broke her pose to jab her finger with urgency in the direction of their guest, and Reuben looked around.

Two large tears were rolling down the writer's face. There was a sound too, Reuben realised.

– I was greatly attached to her and exceedingly valued her friendship, the writer seemed to be saying, but they could hardly make the words out through the poor man's sobs.

This understandably brought a halt to proceedings. Given the man's embarrassment, Gina saw fit to withdraw, and Reuben poured a glass of the Refosco, which the writer did not decline. Reuben stood and looked at him at a loss. At length he decided to make light of the situation.

– I was thinking of bringing this initial session to a close anyway, he informed the writer. I could see Gina beginning to tire.

– Of course, of course. The gown is a heavy material, the writer agreed, wiping his face and brow now with an embroidered handkerchief.

– Do you need me to fetch someone? Reuben asked next.

– If you could escort me to the nearby *traghetto*. Giorgio will be there.

Before going, he went to check on Gina. He was a little startled to find her standing in the middle of the bedroom waiting for him.

– Help me out of this, she demanded, turning her back so he could undo the buttons there. I do not want to wear it any more.

– No. I was just saying how tired you must be. I had lost all track of time. We can restart tomorrow.

– I mean ever, she stated firmly over her shoulder.

Reuben looked at her, a little alarmed.

– Why? Whatever is the matter?

Without replying, she stepped out of the unbuttoned, collapsed shell of the gown and began to rub her limbs as if trying to get some life back into them. Her disquiet was such that she had difficulty finding the English vocabulary to communicate her experience.

– *Mi mancava l'aria*[25], she told him, and when he shook his head indicating his incomprehension, she tried: *Soffocavo*.

– Suffocated? he put to her.

She nodded, and then, waving her hands in an effort to conjure up a better description, she suddenly found the formula and declared, half in English, half in Italian:

– I felt like I was … *annegavo. Sott'acqua.*

Living as he had been in the watery city for some months now, he was acquainted with these terms: she had just informed him that she felt as if she had been drowning.

Before he could interrogate her further, the writer was calling his name.

On their way to the *traghetto*, the writer was obliged to lean on Reuben for support. They proceeded thus in silence until, the gondola in sight, the writer stopped and said:

– I may have been guilty of having once expressed myself clumsily to the Lady, in which I may have appeared to intimate that I was coming 'here' to live.

Reuben held his peace, expecting more. However, the writer unhooked his arm and continued unaided to the boarding point.

Giorgio noticed immediately the agitated state of his passenger and seemed to blame Reuben, for he cast him the blackest of looks, but said nothing.

Returning to his lodgings, Reuben found the studio empty; as he crossed the room to check the bedroom he critically examined the early marks he had made on the canvas. Easing open the bedroom door, he saw the gown concertinaed on the floor and Gina in her chemise lying face down on the bed. She appeared to be asleep. Quietly he reached down and lifted the discarded garment. Gina did not stir. Looking around he located the clothes hanger and took this too.

Shaking it out, he suspended the gown over the chalked cross and went and poured and drank a glass of the wine. Then he spent some time looking from the canvas to the gown before putting down the wine glass and taking up the brush again to continue the work.

Part Four:
Ponte Dei Pugni

1.

Then Gina disappeared.

Having worked well into the night, Reuben woke mid morning, looked around and got out of bed to peer groggily into the open, now empty, drawer in which Gina had been keeping some jewellery, toiletries and combs. The only items of clothing in the wardrobe he discovered were those belonging to him.

He wandered into the adjoining studio, despite knowing it would be empty. He looked around it anyway, and then his eyes stopped on the canvas and he paused to gauge the effect the mid-morning light had on its surface. Reuben was pleasantly surprised to see so much more detail in the picture than he could remember having rendered in the small hours; the picture was coming together, taking shape, almost despite himself.

The family name was Neroni. Reuben's landlady had only the vaguest of notions as to where they resided. So he went off in search of Tito. He found him working in the *cavana*[26] that he rented with his brother-in-law. It was this latter who was able to suggest the *sestiere*[27] to visit.

Finding this district, Reuben enquired of a number of locals, one of whom, when he thought back on the incident, must have circulated the information about the over-inquisitive *forestiere*[28] who had appeared and was asking questions in the neighbourhood.

For, walking past a warehouse, Reuben was roughly manhandled from behind, quite sharply spun around with such force that when let go of he stumbled backwards against the stone wall of the building. In shock he looked up to see a burley assailant, wild shock of hair, ruddy features and fists raised.

Reuben raised his own.

Reuben was not unacquainted with Cashel Byron's profession. Being the son of a local landowner had not made him immune to rough treatment at the hands of the *scológs* and *diúlachs*, the village and farm boys. Many a friendship had come via fisticuffs.

Squaring up now to his opponent, Reuben was vaguely aware of a smattering of onlookers and deduced from their disinclination to intervene that the attack had behind it a motivation other than that of robbing some errant tourist. There was more Venetian than Italian to the words the man was suddenly directing at him, but he thought he heard the name 'Neroni' in the midst of the flow, so he nodded his head and said:

– *Si! Dove casa Neroni?*

This had the effect of inciting the man further, for he was of a sudden lumbering forwards, flailing his arms. Reuben went into protective mode, crouching so his head was protected on each side by his raised hands. Moving forwards to get inside the whirl of the man's blows, he blocked one punch with his left forearm, saw the open channel to the man's face, but held back his right fist as this was his brush hand. So he led instead with the already extended left, which meant a light jarring of the assailant's jawline. This initial engagement had them both blowing hard. They each backed off and circled, Reuben content to be away from the wall in case he found himself pinned against it, though he was wary too of having his back to the partisan bystanders.

Then the pugilists closed again, and Reuben absorbed two strong blows with his upper arms and shoulders. Risking his right hand, he drove that fist into the man's exposed abdomen, and without going down the man doubled over, his hands clamping each thigh to keep balance. He remained like that, retching and short of breath. Reuben circled again and was contemplating his next move when a familiar voice caused both men to pause, his assailant jerking his head up at the sound, Reuben looking around.

Gina came at them, pushing brusquely through the small crowd. Ignoring Reuben she harangued his assailant, and although he could not understand the man's words

Reuben could see the meek defence he was offering by way of excusing the assault. This in no way mollified Gina, who issued a second tirade, further chastening the man. Next she spun around, making Reuben start, and, ignoring him anew, directed her fiery words at those onlookers who had chosen to remain in order to dismiss and disperse them. They now sheepishly dissolved and retreated, though two women put up some token resistance that included waving their hands dismissively and demonstratively before exiting the scene of combat.

With order restored, the man looked around him, saw what he wanted and, retrieving it and dusting it with his hand, returned Reuben's hat to him. Reuben had not realised it had been knocked from his head. Then with one last glance at Gina, the man went off.

– That, explained Gina, was my cousin, Angelo.

– Your cousin! And what cause could he possibly have to attack me so? Reuben demanded.

– He was trying to protect me, she endeavoured to explain.

– What? exclaimed Reuben. Protect you? From me?

Gina looked up at him. He could see how sad she looked.

– Of course not from you, she assured him.

She then elaborated.

– From what is in your studio.

The statement had a more stunning effect on Reuben than any of her cousin's blows.

2.

– Haunted!

Her statement barely commended itself to reason.

It had been a lengthy exchange – in a local hostelry – before this conclusion had been arrived at via the halting, circuitous route plotted by his poor Italian and Gina's slightly better but still somewhat rudimentary English. Now that they were arrived, her whole assertion seemed preposterous to him. However, it was the reason why she was not prepared to don the dress again, why she had in fact packed her things and left.

– *Piuttosto nuda*, she had stated.

– Than wear the dress you mean? He had pressed her on the matter.

Initially she had used the word '*spirito*' to explain her feeling, but she could see in his face the mild confusion caused by this term.

– '*Spirito*'? he had echoed her. Spirit?

Realising he was not grasping fully her meaning, she provided the alternative: '*fantasma*', and watched as it delivered the desired effect.

– Ghost? he corroborated, trying not to make her feel peasant or patronised; hoping she would understand the English. She did.

– *Si*, she assured him. 'Ghost'.

Pondering this revelation, he half-turned away. If he got her meaning right, Gina had just indicated to him her belief that the Lady's gown was haunted, the ridiculousness of which would have mounted for him had he not suddenly been reminded of the book the writer had brought with the dress. To his surprise, he had to admit that Gina, in her elementary fashion, had provided him with a simplified version of the book's theory of psychic energy that its author insisted impregnated walls and surroundings, clothes and belongings to do with the dead.

He turned back to her smiling sadly. He shook his head to indicate that he did not share her superstition. Then he was taken aback, not so much by the lack of angry reaction to his dismissiveness as by the sudden look of pity that suffused her face. She stepped forward and laid her hand gently on his chest.

– You must stop drawing, she impressed upon him. Return the dress to the American; it is his possession. Do not let it become yours.

He made no further attempt to reason with her, impressed almost by how afraid she was. Visualising the half-finished picture, he, however, remained unfazed.

Back in his studio, he reflected how the Venetians, like the Irish, seemed to relish their ghost stories. He went over to the window and, looking out, remembered the story of the House of the Seven Dead Men. At least the version Tito had told him.

Teaching him how to handle the boat, Tito and he had rowed out one hot afternoon far into the lagoon. He remembered how the heavy canal traffic thinned out until there were only crab-boats working the muddy inlets. Each with an oar, they powered the skiff over the seaweedy Vale of the Ditch of Low Water, then the smaller Vale of Above the Wind, winding deeper into the narrowing channels.

Eventually, they allowed the skiff to run gently aground on a slope of silt and they got out a rough and ready luncheon of bread, cheese and red wine. As they rested, Tito informed him that farther along, around the bend, stood the infamous Cason dei Sette Morti. And Reuben was content and amused to lie in the afternoon sun and listen to Tito's tale.

He told how six fishermen, returning to their fishing lodge on the mud flats, came upon a drowned man floating in the water. It was customary to deliver such a grim – but not unusual – find into the city, to the Bridge of Straw, where those with a missing family member would know to go as part of checking the possible fate or whereabouts of their relative. However, as it was late, the six men determined to take the body back with them to the lodge with the intention of taking it to the city the next day. They also, it seemed, determined to play a black-humoured prank on the young boy who cooked for them and kept the lodge in order.

Filing into the lodge they saw that their evening meal was ready to be served, and they informed the boy that they had a guest. They instructed him to go to their boat, where the stranger had fallen asleep, and invite him in to share their repast. One of them called after the boy to shake the stranger well as he was stone deaf. They stifled their laughter as, sometime later, the boy returned, and much to their confusion proceeded calmly to ladle out the food. Then their blood turned cold at the sound of sodden, heavy footsteps on the wooden decking leading to the lodge door, which duly opened, and in walked the pale-blue, bloated corpse.

The six men died of fright there and then, Tito assured him, leaving the young boy to row in the next day and alert the authorities.

– A true story, Tito swore at the end.

Reuben merely smiled and shook his head, much as he had just done now with Gina. Then as now, he hated not having the Italian to tell about his physician grandfather; to explain the enlightened view he had once shared with Reuben with regard to the supernatural.

– The famine, his grandfather had expounded to him, is why the undead are among us here in Ireland. The Greek for deep sleep is 'coma', and people would regularly fall into these. But the poor peasants believed that their loved ones were in fact dead, and they or their neighbours would hastily bury the poor souls.

– Even though they weren't dead? he had asked, aghast.

– The people were not to know this. Now, because they also were starving, they would frequently have only strength enough to scrape out a shallow grave. Often the person laid in it would awaken and manage to dig and scrape a way out of the makeshift resting place. Can you imagine the shock his family and neighbours would get to see the undead walk among them?

Reuben wondered what his grandfather would have made, were he still alive, of 'psychic energy'.

He stayed up late, daubing at the canvas. It was never, he sought to console himself in face of the empty garment, intended to be a portrait: the writer did not seek what he termed 'bald realism'. Indeed, the indistinct features seemed to suit the composition.

At length he retired, worn out. However, at some point during the night he awoke from troubled dreams and found himself transfixed in his bed. He listened to what sounded like the rustling a woman's dress makes when its folds and hemline brush against walls and furniture. Gina? Returned, repentant at leaving him? Eagerly he struck a match, only to find himself the sole occupant of the bed chamber.

The following night, awaking as from a fever dream to the same sweeping sound of a dress, he fumblingly lit a lantern and, raising it aloft, the trembling illumination revealed again the empty room.

In the morning he removed the picture from its perch on the easel. He placed it gently on the floor, angled to the wall with the picture facing inwards. On a whim, he went and heaved the larger canvas of his view of Venice onto the stand. Perhaps as a result of his agitation following a restless night, he inadvertently placed the painting upside down. Noticing this, he went to rectify the situation before being halted by the tilted contrapuntal effect this caused: the capsized Euclidean lines and overturned Cartesian geometry of the buildings draining out from the perspective, becoming suddenly subservient to the swirls and eddies of unfocused shapes and shades and colours, and this composition enthralled him and made him quite dismiss the feverish memory of the nocturnal experience. He was not, he reminded himself, either superstitious or credulous. Something about the liquid nature and fluidity made him lift again and regard afresh the figure he had drawn in the grey gown, and it gripped him anew.

Excited now, not unsettled, he resolved to proceed with the commission.

3.

Colonel William 'Buffalo Bill' Cody on the *Canalazzo*; his right arm frozen in extravagant extension where he has doffed his Stetson in a cavalier flourish of gallantry and showmanship, all captured by the camera while below him in the gondola sit his Indians, one of whom is Red Shirt, chief of the Sioux Nation.

The framed photograph was dated 1890, and it sat as a centrepiece in the window of Signor Grimaldi's shop, just off the *Merceria*. There were other curios in the window too, but it was the photograph that had held his attention and delayed his entering. He had to lean in to read the caption beneath the image. The photograph, Reuben knew, was meant to get more than his notice; it was put there as a lure for the influx of American tourists who, much to Signor Grimaldi's pleasure, were threatening to turn Venice into one big curiosity shop. In London he would have hired one from the artists' colourmen and picture-restoring firm of Robertson and Co., located close to the Royal Academy. In Venice, Reuben was hoping Grimaldi might help him to procure a lay figure.

The interior of the shop was ill-lit and over-cluttered with objects, but he could still see the look of delight on Signor Grimaldi's face when he looked up from where he and his assistant, Fredi, had been checking a large glass bowl for flaws, and beheld Reuben.

– Just the man, just the man, he greeted him, relinquishing the bowl to Fredi and coming forwards to shake his hand warmly and lead him on into the shop. Two people. Two people! he continued, holding up two fingers to emphasise the point.

– Two people? Reuben was intrigued, forgetting suddenly the reason for his visit to the shop.

– Asking for you, Grimaldi excitedly explained. Wait there.

Grimaldi went off behind the counter that took up one side of the shop, disappearing into the back office. Moments later he returned.

– Are they potential clients? Reuben enquired.

– This one I think not so much, Grimaldi said, holding up the pasteboard business card, which Reuben, with some disappointment, recognised.

– That gentleman has left Venice, I believe, Reuben informed the merchant.

Grimaldi merely shrugged his shoulders and crunched up the card; the second piece of paper perhaps explaining his lack of dismay at Reuben's update.

– But this, he enthused, is the name of a young lady who wishes to talk with you. See? She has written her name and the name of the hotel she is staying at. The Hotel Britannia no less.

– And does she want me to paint her?

– She is American, Grimaldi confusingly replied.

– And? Reuben scrutinised the old man's face.

– Americans always want to buy. They rarely have time to remain in one place to be painted. She wants to buy your landscape.

Reuben looked at Grimaldi with a mixture of shock and incomprehension, and observing the look the old merchant wagged his finger in mock admonishment and made a show of directing his words to Fredi:

– What have I told him about wasting time on landscapes? He tut-tutted. There is money in portraits. However, on this occasion I admit I may be wrong. She has heard that you do this landscape and you must go immediately and talk with her.

Grimaldi was suddenly looking Reuben up and down with concern.

– But I cannot send you like this, he berated Reuben, and to illustrate lifted the artist's arm to reveal the sleeve of his coat. Do you wash your brushes with this?

Unceremoniously, he let the arm drop and scuttled off once more into the back of the shop. This time when he emerged he carried an almost new velveteen frock coat, which he coaxed the artist into. Looking around him into the gloom he retrieved a gilt-backed hairbrush next, which he handed to Reuben, indicating a vanity table on which there was affixed a freckled mirror.

– I'm a working artist, Reuben grumbled, taking the brush and going over to the table.

Reuben was taken aback to regard his red-eyed and dishevelled appearance. There were streaks of paint in his normally auburn whiskers; these he picked at to remove them.

– Make the sale, Grimaldi instructed as he led Reuben to the door. And we can take for the coat from that.

It was only when he was outside that he realised he had forgotten to ask Grimaldi about an artist's dummy.

4.

The concierge regarded Reuben for a long time before deigning to send a note to Miss Jones's suite. Reuben waited the while and was unable to stop himself tugging at the cuffs of his sleeves or smoothing the lapels of the new coat. On reading the reply that the bellboy returned with, the concierge's manner changed slightly and he had Reuben shown into a small private salon to wait on the lady's pleasure.

Reuben looked out the window and watched the busy traffic on the Grand Canal, and therefore was unaware of the lady's entrance until she politely cleared her throat. Turning, he found himself beholding a striking young woman; the light outside, coming up off the surface of the water, seemed to brighten her face, the gaiety of which was immediately amplified with the smile she offered him by way of greeting.

– Mr Ross, she was assuring him, it is so kind of you to find the time to see me. I know how busy you are.

Reuben realised that she had the same accent as the writer, and thinking this he was somewhat startled when in the next breath she mentioned him by name. This, he quickly saw, was the solution to the mystery as to how she had come to know about his landscape. Before he could question her further a waitress arrived with a tray of tea, which Miss Jones had taken the liberty of ordering. She instructed the girl to leave the tray and proceeded to serve Reuben herself. While she was doing so she revealed her desire to purchase the painting. Reuben could only for the moment stare. Seeing his reaction, she laughed and handed him his tea.

– You gawk, sir, she informed him.

– With good reason, he was able to return. It seems you wish to buy a painting that you have not even seen.

– Oh, but I have seen it, she brightly replied. Through his eyes. He quite raves about your landscape.

– Really? Reuben said, suddenly eager to hear more.

– Indeed, to call it 'landscape' quite does it a disservice, I'm told. You quite liquefy, it seems.

– I do? Reuben responded.

– He says you make a paint pot out of sunlight and seawater, she continued, obviously enjoying his rapt attention to her words, and that he can hear the muffled sound of distant waves, though one wonders where he heard sounds looking at a picture.

As she spoke, Reuben could see again the close scrutiny the writer had given the canvas upon that first visit to the studio; at the time he had half-wondered if the attention had not been out of good manners, a mere show of interest.

– Well … if you are sure. But I have to inform you that it is not yet finished and I am working on a commission, he felt it only fair to tell the young woman.

And startling him anew, she said:

– The gown, is it not?

– He has told you that too?

– He quite confides in me, she assured him.

The young woman had the ability to disorientate him, and sitting there he felt all at sea. He was rendered all the more rudderless when she announced:

– I will pay for that too.

The delicate cup and saucer almost trembled in his hand. He feared that to refuse her this would jeopardise the sale of the bigger canvas. Nevertheless, he said:

– You cannot, with respect. He has commissioned it.

– I do not mean to buy it, she clarified, merely to pay for it.

As he took this in, it did not really clarify anything. She smiled this time at his confused air.

– Why? If I may be so bold, he asked.

She considered for a moment.

– It is quite bold, she plainly told him.

– Forgive me, he returned. It is quite remarkable, that's all. You must think quite fondly of him.

She laughed aloud at this, though some colour came to her cheeks.

– You think me in love with him, she exclaimed.

He found himself laughing as well, and felt emboldened to say:

– I am quite jealous.

– That is forward, sir, she scolded. In any case, I am to be married next month. In Rome. I intend the painting to be a present for my fiancé.

– Then I am jealous of him, he stated more gallantly.

– He must not know that I have paid for the commission. When he offers some payment you must find the excuse for declining.

– Of course, Reuben assured her.

– My lawyer has drawn up a contract. You may peruse it, and if in agreement with these arrangements you may sign it. I believe the fee cited to be adequate.

Reuben glanced at the paper she passed to him, and at length he took the pen she had ready and signed his name. As he was handing back the contract, and with the powerful voltage of a revelation, the matter suddenly came clear to him, and it quite shook him.

– Good Lord, he exclaimed. Is he bankrupt?

– He is not impecunious, she sternly corrected him, but he lost a great sum when the Barings Bank collapsed. And he has had an unfortunate reversal of fortunes in the theatre. I merely look out for him now and then.

– Are you in some way indebted to him?

She stood up by way of dismissing him. Looking down at him, she at length gave him this in reply:

– Why, have you not read his work? Are we not all of us in his debt?

Reuben stood and reached for his hat, unsure of whether or not the young American was perhaps having a joke at his expense. His uncertainty led him to risk once more the attribution of impertinence, perhaps even impropriety, for he enquired:

– Did you know the Lady?

– Of the gown? she asked, as if gaining time to formulate her response.

To get his answer he had to follow her out into the foyer of the hotel, where he had the distinct impression that the concierge's gaze was trained once more upon him.

– I met her once in Rome. I was more acquainted with her writing. She was a very good writer, although her talent was not the equal of her great-uncle's. I'm sure you've read him.

At this, Reuben looked a little chastened, having to confess that he had not.

– Why, Miss Jones exclaimed with a light laugh at his admission, I thought all young men grew up wanting to be a 'leather stocking'! Perhaps it is only in America.

And now definitively he was dismissed, for she was heading to the stairs to ascend to her quarters, and Reuben was already missing her bright, lemon-coloured laugher. In all he had found this a quite enchanting encounter, and one he was sorry to see come to a close. Deliberately snubbing the concierge, he exited the hotel.

5.

There was something about the incongruity of the image that drew Reuben back to Grimaldi's shop two days later with the intention of purchasing the photograph of Buffalo Bill, for he knew now what he wanted to do with the image. In the days after first setting eyes on it, the composition grew in his mind of an updated, possibly ironic, version of Emaunuel Gottlieb Lentze's vast picture, *Washington Crossing the Delaware.* He was excited at the prospect of reworking and relocating that iconic image of the American Revolutionary War.

It was, however, no longer on display in the window.

His suddenly urgent enquiry as to the fate of the item, on entering the shop, was ignored by Grimaldi's spontaneous rebuke:

– That is not the fine coat I gave you.

Reuben felt his face colour.

– It belonged, Grimaldi was continuing, to a talented young man.

Reuben reacted to this statement.

– And what? he demanded. Were you hoping that some of his talent would rub off on me?

Grimaldi's response to this was a sad shake of his head accompanied by a look of sudden melancholy.

– He died of typhoid fever, he replied. You have not sold it!

Reuben was already befuddled by the absence of the photograph, and this unexpected exchange further confounded him so that, finding himself ill-prepared to supply a plausible falsehood, he told the truth.

He had felt the discreet tug on his sleeve while forging through the crowd on the Rialto. He at first disregarded it, putting it down to the impudence of the new hoards of Baedeker-bearing tourists. He looked around though at a second, more insistent, tug.

– We need to talk, Dalglish said, jerking his head as an indication for Reuben to follow.

Reuben did not include in his account to Grimaldi the mixture of dread and anger he felt in the pit of his stomach at the encounter; the latter in great part due to the interruption he feared to his painting.

Nevertheless, he followed Dalglish, off the bridge and through a tangle of backstreets and narrow passageways until they ducked into the smoke-smeared interior of a tratorria where, even in as pungent an environment as Venice, the reek of fish and vegetation made him gag.

When they got themselves leaning on a small ledge, fastened to one of the walls, Reuben said:

– You're not going to tell me Lynch is still in the city?

– He has tried to leave by train, but the station's watched, Dalglish explained.

Reuben nodded, and then looked Dalglish squarely in the face to inform him about how he had been taken in for questioning. Dalglish took in this information with a growing look of alarm on his face.

– I admitted to knowing Lynch of course, Reuben went on, but denied any knowledge of his current whereabouts. Which is the truth, as he can't be staying at your workshop.

There was something sheepish about the look that Dalglish returned, which made Reuben straighten up and survey apprehensively around them. He was suddenly seeing agents everywhere.

– You mean he is there? Are you insane? They have files, he impressed on Dalglish, and if you say you were involved with activists in Glasgow, they may well have one on you.

– Which is why we must get him out of Venice.

– 'We'?

– You row, don't you? Dalglish reasoned. We need to get him to Torcello. He has a contact there who will take him east.

– I don't want to know any details, Reuben insisted, turning as if to walk out of the premises.

– He's your friend, Dalglish appealed.

Reuben glared in riposte to this, but remained silent for the moment, mulling the matter over.

– I would not be able to row, he said at length. It would need to be done under cover of darkness. But I know someone who might. We would have to pay him, though.

– Lynch tells me he has funds, Dalglish assured Reuben, visibly relieved now to have an ally.

With Tito keeping the skiff steady, Reuben found himself contemplating the worn soles of Lynch's boots as he lowered himself down from the high window at the back of the workshop. He had already tossed down his valise, which was now stowed on board. Once on board himself, he gave Reuben a companionable slap on the upper arm (Reuben winced) and indicated Tito.

– Does he speak English? he whispered to Reuben.

– Not much, Reuben returned.

– And what does he know?

– He knows you will pay him when we get to Torcello.

Something about this statement caused Lynch to laugh out loud, alarming Reuben so that he looked both around them and then back at Lynch in confusion.

– Paying the ferryman, Lynch declared by way of explanation.

– I don't think that particularly amusing, Reuben replied.

There was to be no further exchange as they wended a way through back and side canals; there was cloak and dagger not smoke and mirrors this time on the water.

When they could feel more than actually see the wider expanse of sea, Tito rested the oar and leaned down to extinguish the prow's lantern. Then he rowed them slowly out into the black lagoon.

Although it may well have made for faster passage, Tito had determined that he alone would row, without Reuben's aid.

– One oar, he explained, makes less noise.

So they sat, skimming along in the dark, and there was something hypnotic about the equal intermittence of the stroke of the dipping oar, so much so that Reuben almost drowsed off. It was the interruption to the rhythmic rowing that jolted him alert. Tito had stopped.

Then Reuben heard the bigger boat, or to be more precise, the voices of its occupants, somewhere to the right of them. And the voices momentarily puzzled him; they sounded strangely foreign yet vaguely familiar to his ear. Lynch realised before he did and, close to his ear, whispered:

– English. They're speaking English.

Reuben gripped the side of the boat and listened intently. Any fear that they were about to be apprehended, however, was immediately dissolved when the voices broke into raucous and rude song, and Reuben realised who they were.

– It's okay, he said aloud, though more in reassurance for himself than his companion. They're naval ensigns. They've been on shore leave and must be returning to their ship.

– The British Sea Power, Lynch observed.

Tito had already worked this out for himself, and had resumed rowing.

The main water thoroughfare into Torcello was more river than canal, and suffered worse from silting than those from which they had recently emerged in Venice. Tito knew a landing place, far enough from the town's central piazza to avoid observation, but close enough for Lynch, with a few directions, to make his way there and meet up with his Croatian contact.

As he was about to disembark, he turned to Reuben with one final request:

– Swap coats with me, he urged. I will blend in better wearing this.

He ran his fingers down the lapel of Reuben's frock coat.

– But I have only had it new these few days, Reuben protested. And it may not fit.

– We are the same build, Lynch argued. Sure haven't people always remarked how much alike we look?

Reluctantly, Reuben exchanged coats. However, as Reuben took possession of Lynch's, it seemed to swing at him and something heavy struck his leg.

– Oh, Lynch laughed when he realised. I forgot about that.

Taking his coat back again he withdrew a service revolver from one of its deep pockets.

– A .442 Beaumont–Adams five-shot, he reliably informed both Reuben and Tito, who remained standing in the bow looking on impassively. The squad-man I procured it from assured me it has seen service in Afghanistan. In any case, I think I'll have more need of it than you.

Then, the last Reuben saw of his coat, it was draped over Lynch's shoulder as he waved at them from the wharf before turning and striding off into the dark. Tito was already pushing off to return the two of them to Venice.

His tale told, Reuben looked to gauge its affect on Grimaldi. At length the old man admonished:

– You are a painter. Painters are not revolutionaries.

Waving his hand dismissively, he returned behind his counter. Reuben looked around the shop then, but could detect the photograph nowhere, and eventually he had to ask the old man about it.

– Sold, Grimaldi declared brightly. The very same day I gave you the coat. A gentleman came in, not long after you left to visit the young lady. He bought it instantly; no bargaining or haggling. Typical American.

6.

Reuben was unsure of the status and nature of his relations with the great writer; all the more so as there had been no contact with the older man since the distraught incident in the studio. Although unsure if, after the writer's upset, he still wanted the painting, Reuben had been proceeding regardless.

Reuben knew the location of the writer's lodgings but he had not yet gone there to ask after him. Leaving Grimaldi's shop, however, he was minded to wander in the general direction as if actual sight of the residence would suggest for him a firm line of action.

Uncertainty dogged his steps, slackened his pace, much to the annoyance of the more energised sightseers forced to find ways about his hesitant, meandering progress. For he worried as he walked.

He dreaded that his calling there in person would be adjudged presumptuous; forward. Then the prospect of being turned away unseen, dismissed with some weak excuse delivered by a supercilious servant, quite horrified him. It was why he drew sharply to a halt when, on turning a corner, he found himself regarding the house front in question. Its sudden appearance, its concrete presence, inspired him to no action. He stood and stared as if hoping to decipher some knowledge from the blank physiognomy of the building.

As he turned away to retrace his steps, he just managed to avoid colliding with a tall man, or rather it was this latter whose reflexes performed a sprightly sidestep to avoid such a coming together. The stern glare the man directed at him afforded Reuben sight of the man's face. He immediately recognized him as Dr William Wilberforce Baldwin from the soirée some weeks before.

Reuben had no sooner registered this impression when a new, more alarming one replaced it: the physician, he immediately realised, was aiming his brisk, purposeful pace, bag in hand, in the direction of the very object of Reuben's intense scrutiny. Reuben watched as a serving girl promptly opened the door and then stood aside as the doctor disappeared within.

It was therefore in a state of even greater distraction and consternation that Reuben retraced his steps.

It was the woman's accent, together with the delighted gaiety of her laughter, that awoke Reuben to the fact that his wanderings had ushered him into the environs of the Hotel Britannia, for there before him when he looked up was Miss Jones. She was standing in the company of a tall gentleman at the display window of a jeweller's. The couple exuded a blend of such health and youthfulness that Reuben could only stand and observe this bright display of courtship, for it was obvious, even at his remove, that the two were embroiled in a wonderfully animated, good-natured ridiculing of one another. He, it seemed obvious to the spectator, was indicating some preposterous gaudy item that might adorn her beauty, and she was showing mock-horror at his recommendation. In the midst of this mutual joshing she spied him over her companion's shoulder, and Reuben immediately regretted his discovery, if only because it interrupted the brief cheer of the situation.

Much to her escort's perplexity, she came away suddenly and approached Reuben, who immediately removed his hat. He almost bowed. Laughing as she came up to him, she nevertheless disconcerted him by whispering:

– Not a word.

– Of course not, he replied, but in vague, confused fashion so that she was obliged to say further:

– About the painting, man. It is for him. Remember?

– Ah!

Reuben remembered.

Miss Jones's fiancé had turned and was observing them; she made no move to introduce him, however. But before he could feel slighted by this, an idea had dawned on him: to ask her about the writer's well-being.

– Is he unwell? he eagerly enquired of her.

– Unwell? He was not so last evening at the opera. He was grumpy as he did not rate the performance, but he struck me as being in good health. Why do you ask?

Reuben replied in vague fashion, deciding not to mention what had occurred in the studio. Nor did he make mention of Dr Wiberforce Baldwin. Instead, he managed to change the subject by agreeing a date of completion for the Venice-scape.

Watching Miss Jones return to her fiancé, and him taking her arm and the two of them setting off lightly with the poise and ease of a stately schooner, sails hoisted, colours aloft, setting out to sea, he realised how the brief encounter had wonderfully raised his spirits.

Turning away, he had already resolved to send a written message to the writer. He would include in it an update of progress on the commission, enquire as to the man's health, and make no mention of the currently unoccupied nature of the grey gown.

7.

Reuben sat and gazed upon the barely covered bosoms of the girls of the *Cà Mazzor*.

These girls had never insisted that he take his clothes off; often a mere unbuttoning was enough. Today, however, he was at work and the girls were not. The matron had given them the morning to prepare themselves as another British naval vessel had dropped anchor just off the Porto di Lido, and she was anticipating sailors and marines getting shore leave. Nevertheless, she served Reuben a glass of wine and let him sit quietly with his sketchbook open. As he looked about him he saw how some of the girls were too short, others too plump, and many too big-breasted for the confines of the grey gown. He was also aware of a subtle change in their behaviour. On previous occasions, knowing he was at work, a number of them would have preened and postured before him until, light-heartedly, he would have had to wave them away. This day they still drifted or flitted about, but mostly gave him a wide berth.

At length, a tall, dark-haired girl from Trieste sat down beside him. Her head lolled lazily against his shoulder so that he had to reposition his sketch paper on his lap and comb strands of her hair away from his cheek with his fingers.

– I hear your Gina is gone, she said, that she is working for another painter.

– Are there no secrets in Venice? he asked by way of reply.

– There are no secrets in a house like this, she assured him with a laugh.

Then, rising languidly, she made to stroll off into one of the back rooms, but not before informing him:

– You'll not find anyone willing to take her place, you know.

– And why would that be? he growled. I pay well. Everyone knows that.

But the tall girl declined to answer, merely shrugging her shoulders and moving away with an exaggerated swaying of her hips. As she led him out, however, Mme Merimée confirmed the girl's assertion.

– My girls are very superstitious. It is all I can do to stop them finding religion.

– Are you saying they are frightened to work for me?

The matron was ushering him out the door as if regretting having let him in. She shrugged her shoulders.

– I don't know what I'm saying, she claimed. You must leave now. We are expecting a lot of business this afternoon and we are nowhere near ready.

Then, as he stepped down into the street, she remembered her business acumen and called to him:

– Please come again. But the sketchbook? You leave at home, yes?

As the house was located close to the *Traghetto del Buso*, he boarded a *vaporetto* and, lost in thought, he stood out on deck and watched idly as buildings and wharves reeled by. Some landmark stirred him from his reverie and, suddenly recognising where he was, he disembarked at the next stop and, crossing the nearest bridge, walked back on himself.

He had been to the Norwegian's studio on a previous occasion, and after just a single enquiry off a local he found again the house in question.

His tentative knocking had the effect of pushing open on its hinges the unlocked door of the house. Calling indoors, he got the impression from the faint echo of his voice that the place was deserted: at that early hour, he reflected, the landlady, mirroring the routine of his own, would be at market. Neither artist nor model seemed to be at home, unless – and here he felt a slight pang of jealousy – they were still abed. Either way, he decided to enter.

Vaguely remembering the whereabouts of the studio space in the house, he approached that door and tapped gently on it. No voice challenged or called out, so, turning the handle, he stepped inside.

He was immediately stopped in his tracks, transfixed by what he beheld. He had stepped, it seemed, into another world.

Not Venice.
Not Italy.

He gaped at the pictures he saw there, perched on easels, hung on walls, precariously balanced on pieces of furniture.

Stark, spare, bare-forked and unadorned: figures and images that remained with him when, an age later, he wandered away from the still-deserted house.

They were alien, and yet at the same time somehow prescient and familiar.

Part Five:
Ponte Della Paglia

1.

The first visit came the following afternoon. His landlady leaving Reuben in no doubt that his visitors flatly refused the invitation to step up to the studio, he had to descend to the small reception room where there was a fire lit against the unseasonal cold. He found the two ladies, the writer's sister and niece, standing at either side of the fire-place. Ursula's cold stare mirrored that of her aunt. Barely acknowledging his cheerful greetings, the older lady wasted no time in getting to the point.

– I must insist, sir, that you cease this frankly morbid enterprise you are embarked on with my brother.

– But how is your brother? Reuben enquired.

The lady hesitated as if weighing the consequences of answering his query, one of which would be to extend their colloquy further than she intended. In the event, the younger American replied:

– You cannot imagine the state Uncle Harry was in when he returned from you, she reproached him.

– Please inform him how concerned I have been, Reuben replied.

– And the gown, the aunt said, ignoring his appeal. You would do well to return that.

– I am happy, madam, to comply with all of your requests as long as you can assure me you make them on your brother's behalf.

The aunt glared at him.

– I make them for my brother's good!

– Cannot you see how tasteless the whole affair is? demanded the niece.

– I have merely been hired to do a commission. Who am I to judge?

– For pity's sake, the aunt broke in. As a gentleman, will you not return the item to us? We will pay whatever expense you have been put to.

– I'm sorry, Reuben said. I am entered into a contract with your brother. Only he can terminate it.

In the face of this stalemate, the aunt took them all by surprise by sitting down suddenly in the sole armchair in the room. Composing herself, she looked up at Reuben.

– You like my brother, do you not? You do not need to answer. You must know that we do what we do out of our love for him. When the lady was alive it was broadly and irresponsibly talked about by our countrymen and women, as if it were some prime attachment, which it definitely was not!

– You mean there was talk of matrimony? Reuben sought clarity.

– My brother has always denied anything of the sort, but it did not stop the gossips. We merely want to avoid the potential for any scandal; to distance my brother from any further involvement in the whole tragic affair.

– My dear lady, Reuben responded to her plea, I am not impervious to the reasons for your request, but I repeat: I am at your brother's service, not yours.

The aunt got up at this.

– To think, she said, I vouched for your good character.

– Vouched? echoed Reuben. How?

– The letter that got your release. Who do you think sent it? Will you not give up the gown?

– There must be some other way I can repay you, Reuben appealed.

The writer's sister shook her head sadly, and without a further word left the room, swiftly followed by her niece.

Left alone, Reuben sank down into the recently vacated armchair. He wondered at his own recalcitrance and steadfastness, not a little shocked by the extent of his reluctance to give up the garment in question. He resolved to finish the painting as quickly as possible and return the gown in person to Alicia. As he stood again he wondered how the ladies knew where to find his lodgings, and almost immediately the solution appeared in the mental image of Giorgio. Giorgio, he recalled, knew everything.

The second visit came in the middle of the night.

Some sound or movement from the studio roused him from his sleep. He no longer imagined it to be Gina, repenting her decision to decamp. With a lit lamp he edged open the intervening doors and sidled into the bigger room.

Entering the studio, the light flickered despite the wind having died down outside. In the dim illumination the dress loomed large and wavered. He could not prevent his eyes being drawn to his painting, reinstated on the easel, as the light played effectively on the points of silver and cream he had painstakingly worked into his rendering of the gown's material. There too was the bright oval where he was working on the figure's faint features. Then he remembered why he was standing shivering in his studio at that time of the night, and turned his attention to the rest of the room. Only then did he realise that the door to the landing was open. He knew he had not left it so.

He peered then more piercingly into the darker recesses of the studio, and a jolt of terror coursed through him when he realised there was someone sitting in the ladder-back chair. He quite froze where he stood.

Then on the heels of fear came exhilaration, born of the belief that here at last was the cause of his night sweats and fretful imaginings. Here at last was an answer. In what he intended to be a determined question, but which came out as a hoarse whisper, he addressed the visitor:

– Who are you?

It had the effect of a twig-snap in a frozen glade.

Pandemonium broke out.

As if suddenly electrified, the figure sprang into action.

It quite threw itself at Reuben. With the bound of a beast in the jungle, it hurled itself across the room and Reuben found himself pinioned to the wall. It was a man's grasp he felt around his windpipe. The lantern was loosed from his grip, and before the light extinguished Reuben saw the maddened blaze of the blue-grey eyes that belonged to the writer. Then all was plunged into darkness.

Instinctively, Reuben brought his freed hands up to break the man's stranglehold, at the same time pushing him forcefully back. He heard the animal-like grunting of the intruder, the table overturning and empty flagon shattering and he realised his landlady was up and raising an alarum. As his eyes adjusted to the dark he saw the visitor making for the door; with him there was a sound as of the swishing of a curtain.

The gown was gone.

Swallowing great, painful gulps of air, Reuben ran.

Down the stairs he leapt, running past the affrighted landlady and out onto the quay. Street lamps projected the other's form up onto the buildings on the opposite side of the little back canal. People were appearing at their windows. Reuben ran, and there was suddenly the mad shadow-puppetry of his own elongated figure jerkily mimicking his desperate pursuit.

When his assailant's shadow suddenly vanished from the house fronts, Reuben realised he had darted down a side street. The man was obviously trying to lose him in the tangle of *calli* and *rami*.

Reuben could hear the man's heels hammering on the cobbles of the next street to his right, and he took off down it. Pursuing still the frantic footsteps, he sped left into a narrow alleyway that issued quite abruptly into a small, ill-lit *campiello*[29]. Here Reuben came to a sudden stop; for so had the sound of the footfall he had been following.

Taking the opportunity to catch his breath, he hesitated before proceeding any farther into the little space. Peering into the darkness, he strained his ears in an effort to detect the other's whereabouts, quite sure that his assailant was lurking somewhere in the square.

Moments passed.

Stillness.

Then the colicky wail of a baby from an upstairs room occasioned the lighting of an anxious lantern, and its shaft of light cut into the dark below and flushed his quarry. Reuben spied the form dislodging itself from the shadows and making for an exit on the opposite side of the square.

Unimpeded by other pedestrians at that early hour, Reuben ran furiously, his long legs gathering pace, his arms pushing like pistons. The street they ran down now was wider, and leading, he knew, to the main canal. However, Reuben was gaining on him. The tails of the man's frock coat were billowing out behind him, enticingly within Reuben's reach. And grunting with effort, Reuben drew ever closer until he was within arm's length, and stretched out a hand.

Then he was abruptly upended; quite flung to the ground.

Ambushed. A second assailant had simply emerged from a doorway and barged into him, knocking him to the ground. For a moment the figure seemed to hover over him, and then it sped off after the first. Groaning, Reuben forced himself to his feet and restarted the chase. Stumbling now, the breath having been knocked out of him, he emerged onto the main canal and glared furiously around. He looked in all directions until his gaze was arrested by the dim sight of an unlit gondola plying its late way diagonally across the wide expanse of black water. There was very little other traffic at that hour.

Reuben would have set out there and then, but when he returned to his quarters there was his landlady to placate, neighbours to appease and his own nerves to settle. When, in his studio, he had relit the lantern to survey the upended table and the shattered glass of the empty fiasco he was struck by the change wrought on the painting. The figure on the canvas appeared stricken to his wild gaze. This elongated figure with its vague, oval face and grey gown seemed to mirror his own state of distress and agitation.

2.

The next morning Venice was a sinuous and side-tracking city. To his mind it colluded to lead him astray, for he found himself being misled down the narrow water-canyons of back canals in and out of cul-de-sacs, many of which ended not in walls but water.

When he eventually arrived at the writer's abode, the entrance hall lay open to the world. Trunks sat just inside, awaiting imminent removal. The household was striking camp. Unchallenged, Reuben sidled into the house. A serving girl with dresses draped over an arm barely gave him a second glance as she hastened up the steep, narrow staircase. Stepping deeper into the building, he checked in the open doors of the reception and drawing rooms, all evidently unoccupied. Then he came to a sudden halt, stooping slightly to peer through the French windows he found located at the end of the hallway.

These gave access to a fine example of the abundant but secluded gardens that bloomed, often unseen from public gaze, throughout the watery city, and his eyes fell on the sight of the author sitting on a bench there, his back to the house. Something about the composure of the scene incensed Reuben anew, and without further hesitation he rattled open the glass doors.

Venice is not a fragrant city, and some sensory confusion arose for Reuben from the sudden perfumed freshness of the garden as he stepped down into it; this was added to by the stillness of the man on the bench, who did not in the least react to the racket of his angry entrance. A dawning realisation of mistaken identity grew with each step closer to the bench, and when at last the man turned to acknowledge him Reuben saw a face that bore a striking resemblance to the writer's but with fuller beard and sadder eyes; eyes, furthermore, that he recognised from the frenzied encounter of the night before. Stunned, Reuben stopped in his tracks, at a loss for words.

– 'It is the merit of a general to impart good news, and to conceal the bad,' the man seemed to quote. Do you know who said that?

The man's enquiring look seemed to penetrate Reuben, who could only for the moment stare.

– Sophocles, the man supplied the answer. Now, can you tell me what good Sophocles was at Stone's River or Bull Run?

Reuben stirred himself, determined not to be thrown or diverted by what sounded like random pronouncements that bordered on the maniacal.

– I think you owe me an apology, sir, Reuben countered. And following that, an explanation.

In response the man stood up, the better to regard him, and Reuben took a precautionary step back.

– There were West Point generals on both sides of course; they studied the likes of Mahon and Henri Jomini together and believed in chivalric warfare fought by gentlemen. How wrong they were. *Madmen and jesters.*

– Did you not break into my rooms last night, sir? And attack me? Reuben raised his voice.

– General Grant was no Jominian though. *He* understood. 'War is progressive,' he said, 'because the instruments and elements of war are progressive.'

– I am resolved to go to the authorities, Reuben retorted, irritated by what he deemed diversionary tactics. He was startled, however, to see the man advance and place a large hand on his shoulder before Reuben could react. He leaned in and whispered:

– I went to war with Colonel Shaw and the fifty-fourth. I should have died, but I didn't. However, these eyes have seen so many horrors, witnessed so much carnage: do you really think your 'authorities' give me cause for concern?

Transfixed, Reuben recognised suddenly the sickly sweet smell of absinth on the man's breath; it had been there, he realised, the previous night as well. After a long pause the man removed his hand, giving Reuben's shoulder a friendly pat as he did so, lifting some lint or dust speck from the lapel of Lynch's overcoat.

– I know you well enough, he relented. We look out for Harry, you see. My sister and I. That's all.

As if he had just dismissed Reuben, the man brushed past him and withdrew into the house. Looking after him, Reuben spotted the writer standing at a first-floor window; he had been watching the curious exchange all along. Gesturing to Reuben to remain where he was, minutes later he appeared through the French windows and came down the garden path to him.

– My brother went to the war I did not go to. And it is with him still.

And taking the artist's arm gently in his own, he proceeded to do a slow circuit of the garden.

– You will have no doubt heard of the Fifty-Fourth Massachusetts; the coloureds' regiment? Well, my brother was an adjutant to Colonel Robert Gould Shaw. Surely you have heard of him?

Reuben merely shook his head, allowing himself to be steered like a somnambulist being guided back to bed.

– It was well publicised. By all accounts the regiment's departure was accompanied by a very uncommon Bostonian show of emotions. Very uncommon: banners fluttered, music reverberated, a multitude of breasts bursting with pride as the soldiers marched by. Among them my brother, and with him went Cabot Russell and Thurston Moore and Anson Hemingway. I did not see them go myself as I was laid up with an injury to my back.

At this point in his account the writer stopped. He indicated the garden bench, and they both went and sat down on it. Reuben heard the faint quaver of his companion's voice.

– The next month the regiment was slaughtered during an impossible assault on Fort Wagner in Charleston Bay, with the guns of Sumter playing on them. Heroic, but as seems to be the way with these things, a madness too. Poor Shaw perished. My brother barely survived; he received a wound in his side and a canister ball in his leg. Physical wounds that have gradually healed; yet I fear he is wounded within.

– Did your sister send him to steal back the dress? Reuben had at last found his voice.

– Of course not. I believe my poor brother overheard us quarrel about it and took it into his own muddled mind to retrieve the blasted garment. You are not hurt, are you?

Reuben did not reply. Noting this, the writer drew out an envelope from an inside pocket of his jacket. It contained the fee they had agreed.

– At any rate, I have come to see things from my sister's point of view. She has made me see sense. I no longer require the representation. Do with it what you will. Reuse the canvas if you wish. A palimpsest, is that not right?

Reuben took the proffered envelope, the weight of which when he held it in his hand suggested banknotes were contained within. Then, on the sudden, he quite rose to the occasion by setting the envelope back down on the bench between them.

– I cannot take it, he declared.

– But you must, the writer insisted. I fear I have caused you much trouble.

At this remark, Reuben went higher still.

– To have been able to come to know you pays me.

The writer turned fully around to better regard his companion; the bright beam of grey eyes only faintly veiled by a soft welling-up. Nodding, he reached out and patted Reuben on his arm.

– I'm bound to say that your brother is capable of causing injury, though. It strikes me he *is* a danger, Reuben felt emboldened to declare.

– We are taking action, I do assure you. We leave Venice this evening. We take him to Geneva. A fortnight's spa treatment. And then we go at Dr Wilberforce Baldwin's recommendation to Vienna.

The two men sat a while in silence, until at length Reuben enquired:

– Do you mean to return to Venice?

The writer pondered the question before replying with a sigh:

– No. Not in the foreseeable future.

The two sat again in silent contemplation of this last response. Then, the writer stirred.

– I really must get back to packing. Come. I will show you out.

At the front door the writer suddenly placed his hand firmly on the artist's arm.

– You must not think that I am ashamed not to have served with my brother, or not to have gone there in his stead; to have known the war from too far off.

Reuben made to give him some assurance that such a thought had never occurred to him, but the writer tightened the grip on his arm, alarmingly recalling for Reuben the hand that had been at his throat the night before.

– There is danger, he impressed on the younger man, in what we do, you and I. It is art that makes life, and I know of no surrogate for the force and beauty of its process. To do it right, have no doubt, requires great courage; and sacrifice.

That evening, Reuben watched them go. They did not see him do this. Not even Giorgio at the oar. And his throat tightened at the sight of this waterborne departure.

He watched the sister take her place facing her two brothers, looking alike from the distance. The niece, he knew, had gone off to London days before to stay with younger cousins. As they slid past on the Grand Canal, the writer suddenly rose to his feet, prompted to do so by having caught sight of something, and Reuben had to fight the absurd impulse to step back into the shadows. He was not the cause of the commotion anyway; a woman observing their passage from a balcony had drawn the writer's attention. However, Alicia tugged at her brother's coat-tail and obediently he resumed his seat. When Reuben raised his eyes again he saw that the balcony was now empty.

Part Six:
London Bridge

1.

John Drake found himself standing on the outside again, looking up at a balcony. This time the balcony belonged not to a palazzo in Venice but rather to the neoclassical frontage of Saint James's Theatre in King Street. He watched idly as a theatre usher, gold braid gleaming on his peaked hat and uniform, extinguished the two torches that had been illuminating the facade of the building; the evening's show was now over and the audience dispersed. There had been a performance of *The Prisoner of Zenda* by Anthony Hope, although Drake had not attended it. He was waiting for Reuben Ross to emerge from the side, stage door.

When he had spotted Ross the previous evening he had almost not recognised him. Only when he had returned to his office that night to write up the notes for that evening did he recall the painter from Venice, and a frisson accompanied the memory. However, his curiosity was piqued and it did not take him too long, the following day, to discover that, painting no longer, Ross was working as a set designer at the theatre. It also did not take too long for Drake to decide what use he could make of this situation, hence the reason he was lying now in wait.

Drake had long acquired the skill of knowing how to approach people or hail them without unduly startling them. Nevertheless, Ross startled when he heard his name called out; Drake noted the gaunt look on the face that turned urgently in his direction.

– I do apologise, Drake said, coming across the street to where Ross stood. I didn't mean to alarm you. We met, in Venice.

He stopped short of coming too close to the man to allow him to survey his face.

– Yes. I remember, Ross stammered. It was obvious that he was trying to dredge up the journalist's name from the muddle of his memory. Mr Gosling, is it not?

– Drake, Drake said, a little annoyed. John Drake.

– Drake, of course, Ross agreed. It was five years ago.

– Seven, Drake corrected him. I couldn't believe my eyes when I saw you just now. After all this time. I wonder: would you have time to come for a drink? There's a nice pub just situated around the corner. It'd be just a fine thing to catch up, don't you think?

Drake stood and let his companion mull it over. He seemed to need to look around him as if seeking permission or inspiration from some outside source. Eventually he looked again at Drake and consented, saying:

– Well, just the one.

– This way then, Drake encouraged, heading in the direction of the King's Head.

They stood at the counter and Ross ordered a glass of gin while Drake requested a pint of ale.

– Are you still painting? Drake enquired disingenuously.

Ross shook his head and sipped from his glass before replying:

– Sets and scenery.

And then suddenly he laughed quite tragically and said:

– Do you know I once painted a Venetian scene, and the theatre director told me it didn't look like the real thing? I had to paint a silly caricature in order to satisfy him.

Drake shook his head in a scandalised way.

– And you? Ross suddenly enquired. Do you do theatre now?

Drake laughed at this and took a long draught of his beer. Then he waved his hand at the loud clientele around them.

– I deal still with the theatre that is life, he grandly declared. Each, he continued, standing with the counter supporting his back and looking around him, must play his part.

– And you are always on hand to record it, Ross added, before catching the barman's attention and gesturing in the hubbub to order refills.

Drake turned again to Ross, and this time drew in close as if imparting highly confidential information.

– There is a rumour, he confided in his companion, that certain high-ranking Members of Parliament are courting

– shall we say? – some of the chorus girls. And here he nodded in the vague direction of the theatre.

Ross took a new glass from the hands of the barman and said:

– There are many suitors every night at the stage door, but I can't say I've recognised anyone in particular.

Drake looked a little deflated by this statement, and he lifted again his glass. Then his face brightened.

– Well that's because you haven't been looking, he insisted. But now, as a favour to an old friend, you'll keep a weather-eye out.

And once again the little man seemed to conjure a business card into Ross's hand. In the smoky, sputtering gaslight, Ross peered at it. He could not remember the name of the man's newspaper in Venice, but he was still able to make out that the name on this card was different.

– You've changed newspapers.

– *The Reverberator* is an altogether more illustrious journal, Drake assured him. Massive readership. You'd be doing the public a great service with any information you might pass to me, and what's more there'll be the price of a drink or two in it for you.

Drake drained the glass he had to hand, reached for the new one and raised it in the air, saying:

– For old time's sake.

– Old time's sake, Ross contested. But don't you remember? You failed to make your rendezvous with me in Venice.

Drake put his glass down and was silent a moment, and then, instead of offering an immediate explanation, a different thought came into his head, which brought a sly smile to his face and he said:

– So. You turned up for our little meeting after all? I had thought you might not.

The little man chuckled to himself.

As if changing the subject, Ross told him how he had spoken to the landlady of the pensione.

– She seemed to think it was one of the local ruffians attacked you.

– It was no ruffian. Drake became serious again. He came at me from behind out of the mist, so I did not get a clear view of him, otherwise I would have showed him what for. But as we grappled I got a grip of his coat, and I can assure you it was of the finest material. At one point he seemed to have a walking cane raised over me. I feared for my life!

Drake stopped his account and, turning his attention once more to Ross, saw how he had lapsed into a quiet, contemplative mood. Noticing that he was once more the focus of Drake's gaze prompted Ross to give a response.

– Well then, you were fortunate to avoid serious injury.

– Do you think, I wonder, Drake suddenly put it to him, that our great writer could have hired someone to attack me?

Ross was suddenly finishing his drink and looking at his fob-watch. His head snapped up again at Drake's next announcement.

– I almost proposed as much to him when I saw him recently.

He smiled again, pleased at the effect his words could have on another.

– And when was this? Ross sternly enquired.

– About a month ago. Outside the Athenaeum Club.

– 'Outside,' Ross echoed. You are not then a member?

Drake ignored this and continued.

– I didn't approach him, as it happens. I had other fish to fry that day. But he is a strange one. It's possible there might still be a story there, although his stock has fallen somewhat. His sales, you know….

But Reuben was not interested in the sales of the writer's work.

– In what way strange? he demanded.

– Well, Drake considered. For instance: do you know where he has been lodging this past month or two?

– I have not seen him since Venice.

– In the very same rented accommodation as the Lady who died used to occupy. That's where.

– Perhaps he is looking for letters, correspondence, Ross surmised.

– There aren't any, Drake declared.

– How do you know?

Drake merely looked at him, and in the smeared gaslight cocked an eyebrow. After a moment, he said:

– Seems he sleeps in the very same bedchamber; the same bed. So the serving girl told me. A nice girl….

Ross was suddenly looming over Drake.

– Where is this? What is the address?

– I don't think he is still there, Drake replied, not a little alarmed by the sudden animation displayed by his drinking companion. Ross took out Drake's business card and, turning it face-down on the counter, asked Drake to write down the address.

– I don't have a pen, the reporter confessed.

Ross had a charcoal pencil in his jacket pocket, which he thrust at Drake, who shakily wrote down the address. Looking briefly at the card, Ross nodded, put some coins on the counter and left the premises.

Although it was now quite late, Drake felt the impulse to follow Ross. Leaving the bar, he quickly spotted Ross walking briskly and yet so deep in thought that Drake had no difficulty shadowing him. After some twenty minutes traversing central London, Drake became in no doubt of their destination and there was no surprise when they eventually arrived outside the address he had written on the card: an elegant three-storeyed Regency town house.

Drake remained back in the shadows and watched as Ross, undeterred by the unlit house front, went up the steps and loudly thumped the knocker. The sound could be heard echoing within the building. No light came on in response. No one came down to the door. Again Drake was not surprised, for he had heard that the writer had recently rented a house in the country. As Ross knocked furiously a second time, Drake was wondering if he shouldn't go and inform him of as much when his eyes were drawn to an upstairs window. He stepped forward to have a clearer view, convinced he had seen not just a curtain part but – and of this he later greatly doubted himself and bethought himself of the beer he had consumed – the figure of a woman appearing to look down at the rowdy caller. But the house had resumed its blank countenance, and after a third time Ross gave up his knocking and instead lurched down the steps. He stood swaying in the street, looking up at the house. Drake had hastily retrieved the shadows to watch and eavesdrop. It quite shook him suddenly to hear the painter groan aloud and in a raised voice seem to plead:

– I have come to ask you to leave me in peace!

The house looked on unabashed. Defeated, Ross turned to go, but before he had gone too far he stopped and turned one last time and said:

– You pursue the wrong man.

The following day Drake made a few enquiries, which confirmed for him what he had already known. The writer was set up in his new residence and the town house was currently empty and unoccupied.

When he returned to Saint James's Theatre the next week, he discovered that Ross had resigned his post.

He had gone back to Ireland, it seemed.

2.

Into Sackville Street, as was – although many people were getting accustomed to the new name of O'Connell Street – seemed to come everyone.

Thousands of people: there were cheering crowds and marching bands, ranks and defiles of Irish National Foresters and GAA members with hurley sticks, representatives of the United Irish League and the Ancient Order of Hibernians, people from all over the country recently arrived at the train stations at Kingsbridge, Amiens Street, Broadstone, Harcourt Street and Westland Row; even suffragettes braved the throng, bearing banners such as 'Self-Government Means Government by Men and Women'. The mass gathering overflowed the city centre, with people backed up onto O'Connell Bridge and swelling into Westmoreland Street and D'Olier Street.

Four speakers' platforms were erected for the occasion, with the main stage located close to the newly erected monument to Parnell. It was from here that John Redmond addressed the mass of people, the Waterford MP having devoted his political career to the idea of self-government in Ireland. This day was his annunciation: Home Rule, he believed, was within grasping distance. Appropriately, to begin, the baritone J. C. Browner gave a stirring rendition of the Thomas Davis ballad, 'A Nation Once Again'. The thousands joined in.

Then Redmond stepped forward.

He said:

– This gathering, its vastness, its good order, its enthusiasm and its unity are unparalleled in the modern history of Ireland. In point of numbers it recalls the monster meetings of O'Connell, but never, at the best of his days, did he assemble a gathering so representative of all Ireland as this meeting today.

And he said:

– Every class is represented here. Landlords and tenants, labourers and artisans, the professions of Ireland, Irish commerce, Irish learning and art, Irish literature, are all represented at this meeting.

On the platform sited at the junction with Middle Abbey Street, Joe Devlin, the Belfast-based member of the Irish Parliamentary Party, was the main speaker. His speech was followed by the young headmaster of St Enda's School in Rathfarnham.

Padraig Pearse said:

– Let us unite and win a good Act from the British. I think it can be done.

And he also said:

– But if we are tricked this time, there is a party in Ireland that will advise the Gael to have no counsel or dealings with the Gall (by which he meant 'foreigner') for ever again but to answer them henceforward with the strong hand and the sword's edge. Let the Gall understand that if we are cheated once more there will be red war in Ireland.

Reuben Ross, who was in Dublin to arrange the affairs of his deceased father and was staying at the Gresham, heard the words of the former, while unbeknownst to him, Lynch was listening to the words of the latter.

How Redmond must have thought this day some sort of apotheosis of his political career, how the great assembly would become a defining historical moment, and that date be forever etched into the minds and psyche of the Irish nation: Sunday, March 31st, 1912.

3.

When, in 1733, William Hogarth discovered that the governing body of the Royal Hospital of St Bartholomew was commissioning art from Italy, he insisted on painting two murals for the hospital free of charge. He was determined to demonstrate that English painting was the equal of anything being produced in Italy.

The registrar general was persisting with describing one of the murals to his illustrious guest, although he assured the medical man that he could 'see' *The Pool of Bethesda* quite clearly from memory. The old man was tired now, having just visited and conversed with the Belgian and French wounded. His intention was to return the next day to speak with and endeavour to bring some support or comfort to the British casualties just arrived from Ypres. However, a staff nurse was waiting patiently for the registrar to cease his commentary, and at an opportune moment informed the old man that one British officer had already asked for him by name.

– A literary admirer, the old man marvelled. In all this suffering and depredation. Please, guide me to his bedside.

Gently, the nurse took him by the arm and they entered and proceeded slowly down the aisle of a long ward. Finding the bed, she helped him into the seat at its side and withdrew, informing the patient of his visitor's presence.

– Do not you know me, sir, under all these bandages?

– I am old and quite blind, the visitor explained.

– And I am no longer young and quite blind, the patient replied.

– Both blind then.

– But you do not recognise my voice even? I suppose it has been almost twenty years, the patient surmised.

– Tell me, the old man requested.

– I saw you, the patient revealed, in the gondola with the gowns. On the laguna.

– Ah no, the old man suddenly lamented. My painter friend! Not here. Not blind. Does this war-monster know no mercy?

– They will not know about my sight until they remove the bandages.

– Then there is darkness enough; we will not give up hope, the old man insisted. I will visit regularly and make sure you get the best treatment. I know people.

– I am afraid they ship me home tomorrow.

– Home?

– Ireland.

– Ah yes. Ireland. So you answered Redmond's rallying call. Still trying to unshackle yourself from the Empire?

– You admit then they're shackles, the patient was still able to return.

The old man could be heard chuckling at this.

– An ill-used figure of speech, he replied; then, after a pause: you know I am a British citizen now myself.

159

Reuben admitted to hearing regularly about the writer in the press.

– You caused a stir in America, he said.

– Oh. A stir! I intended it to be a spur rather to get President Wilson to face down these authors of atrocity and ruin. I am mostly condemned by the Yankee press. They call it an act of national apostasy; I am branded either an Anglomane or a traitor.

Then their heads turned in unison at the soft footfall, which was the young nurse coming politely to inform them that Mrs Wharton's chauffeur had arrived to collect the old man.

– Please inform George I will be down shortly, the old man requested. Then to the patient: there are at least some examples of American involvement. I am honorary president of the American Volunteer Motor Ambulance Corps, and I have already heard of an American officer, a Lieutenant Henry, serving in Milan. Also Mrs Wharton is currently in Paris organising American Hostels for Refugees. I've briefly, as you can hear, inherited her chauffeur.

– I moved back to Paris shortly after you left Venice, the wounded man informed him, then London.

– Ah, the old man responded.

– I had to, he explained, for you quite landed me with her, did you not? I got to hearing her footfall in the night, the swish of her gown. Then I realised she was coming to stare at the painting; at the anguished figure I had inadvertently created there.

– I see, the old man said, pondering what he was hearing. You were very young then. Impressionable. I perhaps imposed too strongly on your sensitivities. Alicia did warn me. 'Psychic danger' she called it, if I remember correctly.

– Eventually I had to stop, the younger man was continuing, not paying much attention to the old man, before I went completely mad. I smothered the canvas in white paint. That was when the sound began.

– Sound?

– It was as if it was pleading. Imploring. It reached such a pitch that to save my sanity ... I did what you did.

– What I did? asked the old man, puzzled.

And with George the chauffeur smoking patiently outside, and with the aisles full of noises and men with not enough chloroform clamouring on the floors below them, with the roar and rattle of heavy vehicles coming through the open windows of the long ward and a Bleriot Experimental one-bay tractor biplane growling in the sky, Reuben recounted his last evening on the laguna.

Tito agreed to row this last time. Wrapping the canvas up, Reuben brought along two blocks of wood from beside his landlady's fireplace. When they had rowed to what Tito assured him was the deepest part of the lagoon, he enclosed the weights with the picture and gently lowered it into the water. Both of them were silent as they watched it sink from sight; Tito, he suspected, crossed himself, although he did not see him do this.

– It was only then, he informed the old man, that I understood.

– I don't follow, the writer replied. Understood what?

– What you were doing that first evening. You were not dumping simply. You were not drowning the gowns. It was a type of burial, was it not? A ceremony. A laying to rest.

And at this point he moved his head sharply at the old man's laughter.

– You know, all tragically, all comically, I suppose it was at that.

– And yet you would not leave her at rest, Reuben challenged. Did you not move into her lodgings in London?

The old man received this in silence. Then he gave his reply:

– Oh, I stayed there briefly to satisfy my curiosity. I appreciate to some it may have seemed irreverent and disrespectful, but she would never have thought so. I suppose I might have been seeking some expiation.

– For what?

There was a silence again, and Reuben lay waiting for the old man to have his moment of contemplation.

– For what? For having let her down, I think.

– It was almost as if *you* were haunting *her*, Reuben put it to him sharply.

Then Henry James raised his voice; he may even have stood up.

– Use everything! You're an artist: use everything. No matter what the experience: pain or pleasure, joy or disappointment; heartache, death. Use it. Even war. Use everything, God damn it!

– Is there something the matter here? asked the soft footsteps.

The two of them turned their heads, and the old man seemed to chortle at his vehemence. Then he gave an assurance that all was in order and he saw fit to put an end to the matter.

– In any case, he returned to the patient, it is all over. Finished.

For a time they both remained still and silent, the bandaged patient on his back in the bed; the elderly writer at his side. Then the old man readied himself to leave.

– Perhaps you will still be here when I return tomorrow, he said.

– Do you come every day? Reuben asked.

– I try to; I consider it a duty of sorts, he replied.

As he shuffled away – Reuben listened to the ringing tap from the ferrule at the end of the old man's walking stick on the cold tiles of the ward and the sound of a nurse walking down the aisle to offer the gentleman some assistance – the writer paused on a whim and, turning in the direction of the patient, said:

– You see: I do my war service at long last. I hope my brother would be proud.

After the writer's departure, Reuben lay a while waiting and when, at last, the hushed footsteps returned, he moved his head in their direction to say:

– I would have called him back, only he sounded so frail. Therefore I did not.

Then Reuben proceeded to explain it: how for one time the old man had been wrong; how it was not all over, it was only at its beginning; and his voice floating down the narrow aisle startled the young nurse on duty, causing her to look up from her station, inquisitive, and crane her neck and strain her eyes to peer into the long and darkening ward where for the briefest of moments she imagined she saw a second, this time unannounced visitor; and these were not permitted.

For as he talked, even now, beneath the bandages he could still see the pale, emaciated famine-figure he had fashioned on the canvas; he saw the maw in the middle of its anguished features from which the sound had first issued, faintly reverberant, back then in Venice, too diffused for him fully to attend, but whose fragmentary atonal strains he began to pick up periodically and recognise in the intervening years, building, growing, only each time with increased pitch and fuller volume, more insistent until, thrummed now on the tuning fork of warfare, he knew it no longer haunted him alone, it no longer deafened him alone, having heard it finally at its most piercing and unmistakeable, perforating the chlorinated fog of gas in Belgium while his men groped and gagged around him and the air whistled with steel and iron ate the earth.

It was the sound of this new century, he would have told the old man.

For all to see.
The scream.

164

Acknowledgements

I am most grateful to the following people: Frank Costello for his support and encouragement; my brother, Brian, for seeing the potential in the mere germ of a story and accompanying me to the Veronese exhibition; and a particular *grazie mille* to Alessandra Chiodelli McCavana. I am also indebted to my two astute editors at New Island Books, Dan and Justin.

While some of the incidents in this story are made up, others are not. Therefore, here are some of the books I found useful when doing my research:

Venice by Jan Morris (Faber & Faber, 1993);

Henry James – The Imagination of Genius by Fred Kaplan (The John Hopkins University Press, 1999);

A Private Life of Henry James by Lyndall Gordon (Vintage, 1999);

Portrait of a Novel: Henry James and the Making of an American Masterpiece by Michael Gorra (Liveright, 2013);

Why the North Won the Civil War edited by David Donald (Touchstone, 1996);

Redmond: A Life Undone by Chris Dooley (Gill & Macmillan Ltd, 2015);
Across the River and Into the Trees by Ernest Hemingway (Jonathan Cape Ltd, 1950); and
The Master by Colm Tóibín (Picador, 2004).

Endnotes

1   *Lezeoni di voga* (p. 4) Rowing lessons.

2   *Felze* (p. 4) The cabin of a Venetian gondola

3   *Fórcola* (p. 6) A typical Venetian rowlock used by the gondolier to control the movement of the oar.

4   *Flâneur* (p. 8) A stroller

5   *En Règle* (p. 9) In normal or orthodox fashion.

6   *Poli* (p. 15) Mooring posts for gondolas.

7   *Traghetto* (p. 15) A gondola ferry station.

8   *Squeri* (p. 16) A Venitian shipyard.

9   *Calle* (p. 16) A narrow street.

10 *Campi* (p. 18) Plural of *campo*. Square. It originally meant a field or plowed area.

11 *Approdo* (p. 20) Landing place, typically a flight of steps.

12 *Fondamenta* (p. 20) Pedestrian walkway on the bank of a canal.

13 *Andare por le fondere* (p. 29) To wander aimlessly.

14 More *brocanteur* than *antiquario* (p. 30) A *brocanteur* is a dealer in second-hand goods; an *antiquario* is a reputable dealer in antiques.

15 *Ferros* (p. 48) Plural of *ferro*, the metal adornment on the prow of a gondola.

16 *Pali* (p. 48) A variation on *poli*, the mooring post for gondolas.

17 *Madonnetta* (p. 48) A collective term for depictions or statues of the Madonna.

18 *Ramo* (p. 55) Alleyway.

19 *Sottoportico* (p. 55) An arch-like passageway.

20 *Sandoli* (p. 63) Traditional flat-bottomed Venetian rowing boats. They are simpler in design to the more famous gondolas.

21 *Spingarda* (p. 63) A punt gun, a long gun used for waterfowl.

22 *Flou* (p. 66) Indistinct, impressionistic.

23 *La Serenissima* (p. 69) A nickname for Venice meaning 'the most serene'.

24 *Carabinieri* (p. 78) Police officers.

25 *Mi mancava l'aria* (p. 88) I cannot breathe.

26 *Cavana* (p. 93) A boathouse.

27 *Sestiere* (p. 93) One of the six districts that make up Venice.

28 *Forestiere* (p. 94) A stranger or foreigner.

29 *Campiello* (p. 134) A small square.